Substantial Fortune

A Parable About Greed and Self-sacrifice

Book 1 of the Keys of Ehadreon:
The Violet Key

DEAR JOSH —

LIVE FOR THE GLORY
OF THE HIGHEST ONE!
IN CHRIST,
PASTOR STEVE

Steve Carlsen

Steven J. Carlsen

ISBN 978-1-64003-882-0 (Paperback)
ISBN 978-1-64003-883-7 (Hardcover)
ISBN 978-1-64003-884-4 (Digital)

This book is a work of fiction. Any references to biblical events, people, places, or symbols are used fictitiously, figuratively, or symbolically. All other names, characters, places, and events are products of the author's imagination, and any resemblance to actual events or places or persons, living or dead, is entirely coincidental.

All Scripture passages are the author's own translations or paraphrases of the New Testament Greek text that is available in the public domain.

Covenant Books, Inc.
11661 Hwy 707
Murrells Inlet, SC 29576
www.covenantbooks.com

To my wife, Ruth.
She is my Sasha and my Tasca.
To everyone else, she is Lady Elaine.
For the glory of the Highest One!

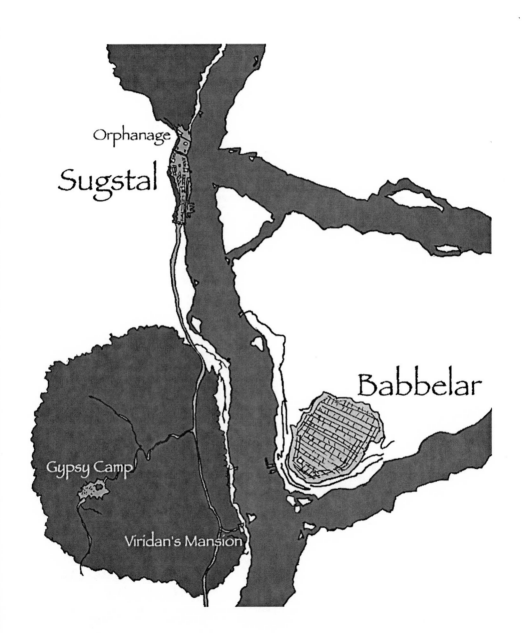

Pure and faultless religion in the eyes of God the Father is this: to provide for orphans and widows in their distress and to keep oneself from being contaminated by the world.

—James 1:27

CHAPTER 1

The Empty Basket

In another place and time much like our own—yet quite different from our own—a brilliant violet light defied the darkness. The light shone from a sword slung over the shoulder of a young gypsy. As she trudged through the deep snow back to her wagon, Sasha felt cold, hungry, and tired. The coat she wore did little to protect her against the bitter cold. Her hands and feet were numb, and her face stung from the bone-chilling air. The sword on her back felt heavier than it usually did, and it just added to her feeling of being overburdened.

She unlocked the door of the wagon, and dropped her basket and sword on the floor. She pushed the door shut against the frigid night and lit a small oil lamp. The silver bands on each of her wrists reflected the light of the lamp all around the interior of the wagon. Ancient runes on each of the bands glowed brightly in the darkness. She lit a wood fire in her small stove, and when the room began to warm up, she took off her coat and hung it on a peg by the door. She took off her boots and socks and put them in front of the stove to dry. Then she slipped her feet into her old, worn slippers and wrapped herself in a thick, hooded sweater.

Sasha looked down into her basket to see what was left to eat. There was nothing but a small piece of bread. Her basket had been overflowing with food when she left the village of Sugstal, but she had given most of what she had to the orphans who lived on the northern side of the village. She had given everything else to the old widows and children here in the gypsy camp, south of the village. She had hesitated for a moment before giving the last of the lamb stew to little old Hala in the wagon next door; but how could she say no to the old woman when she looked so frail and hungry?

As she held the small piece of bread in her hands, her stomach grumbled. She had hardly eaten anything at all that day. She sighed deeply, gave thanks to the Highest One, and slowly began to eat the bread, washing it down with some water from a small tin cup. It was not much, but a least she could comfort herself with the knowledge that she would get a good meal the next day at the tavern where she worked as a waitress. Still hungry, she climbed into the bed. She wrapped herself in a thick blanket, laid her head down on the pillow, and struggled to fall asleep in the bitter cold.

After tossing and turning for a while, Sasha looked up into the darkness and prayed. "Why is it such a struggle? Why do so many go hungry while others throw food away? Why should I be so cold, while others have warm houses to live in? Why do us gypsies live in complete poverty, while the people of Babbelar throw money away on things they don't really need?"

Sasha began to wonder if all her efforts to bring food to the people in the camp was really worth it. After all, those she helped to feed one day would just be on the verge of starvation again a few days later. The battle to have enough to eat was unrelenting. She began to be filled with a sense of despair, and she cried herself to sleep.

Outside, in the darkness, a large woodsman materialized out of the shadows by the tree line. As he ran toward Sasha's wagon, he unsheathed the large sword that was slung over his right shoulder. The blade blazed with a brilliant, blue light. He tossed the sword in a perfect arc toward the top of the wagon, and the light revealed five large lizards crawling on the roof. They hissed and cursed as the sword ran right through one of them. The lizard exploded in a puff of black smoke. The other four lizards scurried down off the roof. The woodsman's sword came flying around back into his hand as he approached the wagon.

One of the lizards started whirling its heavy, black chain around its head. It hurled the chain in the woodsman's direction, but he easily jumped over it. He slashed at the lizard with his sword, and it vaporized into smoke.

Another lizard then jumped on the woodsman's back and started choking him with its black chain. The woodsman flipped his sword around with one hand, and brought the blade down fast along his right side. It plunged deep into the *nekron* on his back. The lizard made a little hissing noise, and then it popped like a balloon.

The other two lizards started running toward the trees. The woodsman tossed his blade into the nearest one's back, and it disappeared in a cloud of dark smoke.

The woodsman placed his hand on the side of Sasha's wagon. On his wrist was a golden band with ancient runes on it that blazed brightly in the darkness. "Be at peace, daughter of the King!" he said. "Do not let your heart be troubled! Rest easy and sleep well! Your labor is not in vain!" Then he ran swiftly into the woods in pursuit of the last lizard.

Sasha woke up as the battle was taking place, even though she had no idea what was happening outside her wagon. At first, she felt more troubled than before, but then a warm sense of peace flooded over her heart.

It was foolish of me to question the Highest One, she thought. "Please forgive me for doubting you," she prayed.

She smiled and pulled the warm blanket back over her head and closed her violet eyes. She fell into a deep, restful sleep in her cozy little wagon. She did not have a worry in the world. Tomorrow she would bring more food back to the camp. No one would go hungry.

* * * * *

In a wagon nearby, a large muscular man with a scar on his face and red eyes noticed that a sense of serenity had fallen over the gypsy camp. In the past, Stang had been a bloodthirsty pirate captain, but now he was the leader of this small band of gypsies. A dark red and black chain ran from one of Stang's wrists to the other under his black shirt and black leather jacket. He usually lived with a constant sense of guilt because of his violent past. But tonight, for some unexplained reason, his conscience seemed to be at ease.

Stang heard people laughing and singing to accordion music in the other wagons and tents, so he went outside to see what was happening. There, around a fire, sat several women and children laughing and feasting on chicken and dumplings. They all had big, greasy smiles on their faces.

"Hello, Mr. Stang!" one of the little girls shouted. "Would you like something to eat?" she said, holding out a half-eaten chicken leg.

As Stang walked over to the fire, the women and children suddenly became very quiet. He looked very intimidating in his dark leather jacket, and he always seemed to have a perpetual scowl on his scarred face. The children began to hide behind their mothers' skirts. The mothers lost their smiles and began to look very frightened. They all knew of Stang's reputation for brutality.

"No, thank you," Stang said quietly. He saw the terror in their eyes, and he realized that he was ruining their happiness, so he said, "Please don't let me stop you from enjoying your meal. Good night."

As Stang walked away, he thought he understood why things were so tranquil throughout the camp that evening. Sasha must have given food to everyone again. Whenever she did that, his nagging sense of guilt would go away, but he did not understand how the two were connected. Nor did he notice that the snow had been cleared around Sasha's wagon, and a patch of small violet flowers called *Ehadre-el* were now growing there. He did not see the evidence that King Tavon's servant had fought a battle there that evening, nor did he know that the nekron had been defeated.

CHAPTER 2

The Windship Yard

Bensareon awoke from a nightmare with a jolt. He sat up in bed in a cold sweat and rubbed the middle of his forehead. He had a raging headache, and he felt tired in spite of sleeping for eight hours. This was the second night in a row he had terrible dreams about losing all the men in his unit in a battle in the Darklands. Feelings of total defeat and hopelessness haunted his mind.

He stood up and looked across the room. Something was wrong. Something was present there with him. Out of the corner of his eye, he saw a gray shape slither into the corner by the door and fade into the darkness. He grabbed his sword, and it immediately began glowing with an indigo light. The light of the blade exposed a snake-like creature cowering in the corner. It was about three feet tall, standing on its hind legs, and held a black rusty chain between its two front paws.

"Despair! Despair! You are a complete failure!" it snarled at him, blinking its eyes because the light injured them. It made an attempt to swing the chain in Ben's direction. "You will always be haunted by utter failure—always," it hissed.

Ben shouted, "I live for the glory of the Highest One, not my own!" as he threw his sword at the creature in a fluid motion. The blade hit the lizard square in its chest. The lizard screeched in pain and vanished in a puff of black smoke. "Wretched worm!" Ben said out loud to himself. He hated how a nekron could rob him of his sleep and steal away his sense of peace so easily.

Ben and his family lived in the small village of Sugstal in the nation of Spysar. Since the entire surface of Varden consisted of rocky crags and steep, narrow glens covered with ice and snow, Sugstal was built on a long, narrow ledge on the side of a cliff, like most towns and villages in that world. The ledge was only five to seven hundred feet wide and about a half-mile long. Shops and homes were tightly packed on either side of the gravel road that ran through the center of the village. They called the road High Street, because it was perched high above the fjord on the eastern side of the village. Low Street was just a rocky path that led down from the village to the docks on the fjord. From time to time, the stone face on the edge of the ledge would give way, and a house or a shop would slide off the cliff and crash down into the waters of the fjord far below. That was why buildings further away from the bluff cost twice as much as those right on the edge of the cliff.

Since he was now restless, Ben put on his windship captain's uniform, slung his sword over his shoulder, and stepped out into the dim morning light. It was a quiet, cold dawn in Sugstal, but then it was always quiet and cold in that part of Varden. It was snowing lightly, and the flakes seemed to float upward on the faint breeze. High Street was empty, except for a man walking toward the windship launch owned by Ben's father. The man stepped into the light just as he walked up to the door, and Ben recognized his brother, Nathan.

"Hey, Nate!" he called out, as his brother opened the door.

Nathan stopped and turned toward his brother. "Did you hear the news? Ebesian and his top students are on their way here. They should be arriving by windship tomorrow morning."

"No, I didn't know that," Ben mumbled.

"Pap said they are going to need a crew for 'an extended adventure.' That means good news! We will have work for months, my brother!"

"Ah—who is coming with them?" Ben asked quietly.

"Ah ha!" Nathan shouted, as he slapped Ben on the back. "Yes, *she'll* be there, too!"

"Really," Ben said flatly.

"Really!" Nathan teased. "It's so hard to love a princess from the house of Saren, especially when she doesn't even know you exist."

Seeing his brother's pitiful expression, Nathan relented and suddenly felt sorry for Ben. He realized he had gone too far in kidding him. He tried to lessen the blow and said, "Aw—you'll be all right." When he saw Ben did not seem to be all right, he quickly changed the subject and said, "Come on, Pap is waiting for us."

They walked into the windship yard's main wooden building. They stepped into the small reception area with a fireplace, four wooden chairs with rosemaled seats, and a long counter. Behind the counter were neatly placed ledgers on shelves. The counter itself was just a large, thick slab of wood from some ancient tree. It was rough-hewn and it still had some bark on the edge. On the counter was a worn, open logbook and a calendar. Ben checked the logbook and saw his father had written *loremaster Ebesian + 6* in the log for the next eight weeks. They walked through the door behind the counter into a large room with a high, three-storied ceiling. A windship sat on rails in the middle of this space, and a gray-haired man was on its deck, working on some of its rigging.

"The ol' *Gullsmear* isn't what she used to be!" the gray-haired man said. Ansen, their father, was the most prominent windship owner in the country of Spysar. The family owned a line of twelve windships of varying sizes and speeds. Their favorite ship, the *White Eagle,* was nicknamed the *Gullsmear* because of the way it seemed to always hit birds as it took off from the ramp at their building on the coast of Spysar.

"She'll fly like the wind!" Nathan said confidently to his father.

"She'd better! Ebus will never speak to me again if she doesn't do what she's supposed to." Ebus was the nickname everyone used for loremaster Ebesian when he was not around. No one would ever call him Ebus to his face. Once a student had done so, and he was soon looking in vain for another loremaster to train him. One thing Ebesian would not tolerate was disrespect. So everyone respected him, because he was, after all, the most knowledgeable loremaster in Varden.

"Ebus will be arriving from Rothal in the morning along with six of his brightest in tow," Ansen said. "I want you to get the charts ready for Ansar down to Bandar. They will probably be going to Kalendore and Samar as well."

Ben walked over to a large cabinet and began looking for the maps and charts of the areas his father mentioned. Nathan climbed on board the windship and began testing the navigation equipment and engines. Ben went to the helm with all the charts in his arms. He placed them on the chart table and looked out the bridge windows toward the bow. As he ran his hand across the helm, he began to experience the old feelings of pride he always felt when he was on board. *There is just something amazing about a windship*, he thought. *It's a beautiful thing!*

The *White Eagle* was especially beautiful. It had twin hulls made of acacia wood, light yet strong as iron. On a deck, extending between the two hulls, was a large pilot house enclosed on all sides by walls and windows, so that the crew could see in all directions from the bridge. It also had a large, triangular, canvas sail stretched over a wooden frame. The sail tilted vertically when it sailed on the water, and horizontally when it flew through the air. Its engine pulled it through the air by interacting with the magnetic fields of Varden. Few understood how it flew, how to keep its engines operating, or how all its complex system of ropes and rigging worked. This is why Ansen and his sons were held in high regard, especially by members of the High Council, who often needed to travel quickly across a world like Varden with its impassible mountains and icy fjords.

fjord

CHAPTER 3

The Broken Window

The next morning, on the other side of the fjord, a three-foot-tall lizard and an enormous toad clung to a rafter in the corner office of Arborax Industries in the city of Babbelar. These were not like the small, dumb, short-lived creatures we find in our world. These were highly intelligent beings that had lived for thousands of years, and they had the power to influence people's hearts and minds, and tempted them to do what was evil. They were once tall and handsome creatures, but millennia of bondage to wickedness had so corrupted their minds and bodies that they had become more and more reptilian or amphibian in appearance. On the planet of Varden, they were called the Nekron. These two nekron hid in the darkness and shadows of the rafters as they looked down on their latest victim. With sinister smiles on their faces, they gleefully poisoned his mind with thoughts of despair and hatred.

"All is lost!" croaked the toad to its victim below. "All is lost! I've lost everything. Gree-dee, gree-dee. It's all gone!"

"I want to kill them!" hissed the lizard. "They deserve to die a slow and painful death for what they've done!"

The toad and the lizard looked at each other and laughed maliciously over their prey. The object of their attacks was a rotund, middle-aged man sitting at a large, mahogany desk. He looked like a frog, with a heavy, round body and spindly arms and legs. His warty face with large jowls resembled that of a toad. His large mouth was cast into a permanent frown. He was dressed in a green, plaid suit that brought out the color of his yellow-green eyes. A heavy, rusty, yellow-green chain hung down from both of his wrists. He was the chairman of the board and president of Arborax, Arboron himself.

Arboron thought he was about to become the second wealthiest man in the city of Babbelar, but now he was close to bankruptcy. He had harvested every single tree on every property he owned. The sale of the trees had made him a very rich man in a world where wood was scarce. Since nothing was left on his land, he had invested almost all of his liquid capital in a "get rich quick" scheme. The scheme was designed to offer bogus investment opportunities to low-income pensioners. Arboron had just been told that the men behind this ruse had been arrested, and all of his money, along with that of many other investors, was lost. He wanted to murder the men who had swindled him. Now filled with rage, he found it was impossible for him to think about anything but getting revenge.

He hoisted his flabby body out of his desk chair and waddled over to a cart covered with bottles near the large plate-glass windows of his office. He poured himself a drink and sipped at the amber liquid. He stared out the window toward the magnificent view of the fjord, but his eyes did not register the beauty and majesty of the mountains, the waterfalls, and the sea before them. He threw his head back and swallowed his drink down in one gulp. He scowled even more intensely, and then he threw the glass in his hand at the fireplace on the other side of the room. As it shattered against the stones, he felt his anger subside for a very brief moment.

"What am I going to do now?" he asked himself out loud. He pounded his fist down on the cart, and all the bottles clinked together. One flask broke and the liquid ran down onto the carpet. Arboron gritted his teeth in a rage, and he threw his skinny right arm across the top of the cart, sending most of the bottles smashing to the floor. Searing pain shot up his arm, and he cursed under his breath. Weeping, he slumped down on to the floor and fell back against the cart. His immense weight slammed the cart against the window, and the large windowpane cracked as the corner of the cart crashed into it. The entire eight-by-ten feet window shattered, and glass shards came raining down on top of Arboron. He screamed out loud as if

16

he was being tortured. The broken glass cut the top of his head in several places, and blood flowed down the front of his frog-like face, making him look even more gruesome. The lizard up in the rafters hissed with laughter, and the toad next to him croaked in glee.

Arboron's secretary burst into the room. She was half Arboron's age and half his size, but just as round as he was. She was dressed in a pale green business jacket and skirt, and she had bright yellow hair that matched her yellow eyes. A yellow and green chain was draped over her tiny shoulders, and she had a face like a young calf. "Are you all right, Mr. Arboron?" she asked, looking around. "I thought I heard a terrible noise!"

"*Yes*, I'm fine, Bovina!" he growled as he lay on the floor. "I told you not to interrupt me. Now get out! *Get out!*"

Bovina was frightened and stunned. She looked around at the glass on the carpet, the broken window, and her boss covered in blood on the floor, wondering what to do. "Do you need help, sir?" she mumbled, biting the fingernails on her right hand.

"*No!* I told you to *get out! Leave!*" Arboron shouted as he struggled to stand to his feet.

Bovina trembled from head to toe, and then meekly turned around and scurried out of the office. As she slammed the door shut behind her, she thought she could hear laughter and the rattle of chains coming from up near the ceiling of the room, but she knew that was impossible. She realized the sound she heard must have been her boss weeping bitterly as he lay in a bloody heap on the floor. She ran out of the office in search of a doctor—not for her boss but for herself. She felt very faint, and she thought she was going to be very, very sick.

CHAPTER 4

The Professor's Inglenook

Loremaster Ebesian was an old man with light-gray eyes, a long nose, and large ears. He had a long gray beard, and his long gray hair was tied back in a ponytail. He wore a gray robe almost the same color as his eyes. He sat alone in the inglenook by the fireplace in his apartment. It was a small place crowded with books and maps. He often thought about moving elsewhere, but he realized he could never find another place that was as comfortable in the center of the town of Rothal, close to the Lore School where he was a professor of theology. Leaning against the fireplace was Ebesian's large sword. It glowed with a soft, white light that illuminated the worn Lorebook in the old man's hands and the silver bands on his wrists.

Ebesian closed the book in his lap and placed it next to himself on the bench. Then he let out a long sigh. He was feeling very grumpy because he was consumed with thoughts about how old he had become. His joints hurt in his knees and his fingers. His vision was blurry after reading for long hours. He was tired, and he sighed with fatigue and weariness. He stroked his beard and rubbed his aching eyes. Then he grabbed his staff and raised his old body up to a standing position. The effort caused an electric shock to shoot down his spine, but he felt all right after he straightened up to his full height.

"What am I thinking to go on an adventure at my age? I must be totally daft!" he said out loud. Just then, there was a knock at his door. "Come in! It's open!" he shouted.

In walked Ebesian's life-long friend, Mandar. "So, are you excited, old man?" he asked, as he took a seat in the inglenook.

"Thrilled!" Ebesian spoke the word with bitter sarcasm. He poured hot tea from a teapot into two mugs on the kitchen counter.

"Aw! Would it kill you to actually enjoy things a little bit?" Mandar asked with irritation in this voice.

"It probably would at my age!" Ebesian carried the two mugs over to the inglenook.

"I'm just as old as you are, you old fart, but you don't hear me bellyaching about everything!"

"You sound like you're complaining pretty well right now!" Ebesian said sitting down across from his friend in the inglenook. He handed him one of the mugs and kept the other one for himself.

"Well, I'm excited! Even if you're not!" Both men drank from their mugs.

"Are the students ready?" Ebesian asked, changing the subject.

"Yes, they're all down at the launch ramp, waiting for *you*."

"The windship doesn't take off for another hour!"

"I know, but they're *excited*, so they got there early!" Mandar explained, lifting up his hands in front of him on the word *excited* to emphasize it.

"All this *excitement* isn't healthy!" Ebesian said, sitting back and sipping his tea. "It sets a person up for tremendous disappointment when things don't go the way they hoped."

Mandar just shook his head. "You're such a pessimist! Why do I put up with you?"

"I give you balance, my friend! Where would you be if I didn't bring you back to reality every once in a while?"

"Well, the reality right now is that your students are waiting for you at the windship yard!"

"Tell them I'll be there just as soon as I pack a few books and maps."

Mandar got up and walked toward the door. "I'm still excited, and I think you are too, but you just won't admit it."

"Go tell them I'll get there as soon as I can."

"Don't be late!" Mandar said, as he walked out the door and closed it behind him.

When Ebesian was all alone, he walked over to the small safe hidden behind a picture on the wall. He dialed the combination and removed all the money that was in it. He placed the few thousand kroner he had in a leather bag, snapped it shut, and placed it on the floor by the door. He hoped it was enough to fund the expedition they were about to embark upon. It was his entire life savings. If he survived the adventure, he would have nothing left to live on, but he was not expecting to come home after it was all over.

Ebesian placed a few books and maps inside another bag with his clothes. He picked up the old Lorebook on the inglenook bench and placed it in the bag as well. Then he slid his sword into a scabbard and carried it and the second bag over to the door. There he slipped on his favorite, old overcoat, and he stuffed a puzzle box into his pocket. He threw the sword over his shoulder, and he turned to look around one last time at the tiny apartment. A tear came to his eye. He wiped it away with the back of his hand, and then he picked up his bags and locked the door behind him as he went out. *His students were excited,* he thought, *and he was about to fulfill his destiny. How often does that happen?*

CHAPTER 5

The Green Tower

At the center of the city of Babbelar stood a tall green tower. It housed the offices of the Ministry of Finance. It was built by the Babbelarians because they wanted to make a name for themselves. That is why it was called the Renown Tower. It was the tallest building in all of the Westlands, and the Babbelarians were quite proud of it.

At the very top of this tower, Capitalo sat in his huge office. The room had windows on all four sides so that he could easily see all of Babbelar from his large, teak desk in the center of the room. From this high position, Capitalo felt like he was the king of all of Varden. He was the minister of finance and the wealthiest man in all of Corasar. He had the same frog-like appearance as Arboron, only his head was larger, and his hairy eyebrows were fixed in a permanent scowl. He always smoked big fat cigars that filled his office with thick green smoke. The heavy, rusty yellow-green chain around his neck was the largest borne by anyone in all of Corasar.

Capitalo had accumulated his vast fortune by deceiving his rich friends with "get rich quick" schemes and robbing his poor laborers of their fair wages. He was heartless and ruthless when it came to money. He was also brilliant when it came to setting up others to take the fall for all of his criminal activities. He had just pulled off his greatest financial scam ever, and the people he used to accomplish it were now about to take the full blame by going to prison for a very long time. He was so cunning that no one even knew that he was the mastermind behind the scheme, or that he had transferred all of his ill-gotten gains to a bank on an island far south of Corasar. No one, that is, except for the true Highest King.

Arboron stormed into Capitalo's offices at the top of the Renown Tower. He wanted to get his money back. He had to get it back, or he was totally ruined. Since he was still covered in his own blood, he frightened Capitalo's secretary so badly she fainted when he came into the room. Arboron marched right over the secretary's limp body and went straight into Capitalo's office.

"I demand that you return all of my investment immediately!" Arboron shouted, pounding on the huge desk.

Capitalo sat back in his chair and calmly said, "I wish that I could do that, my friend, but I can't. These swindlers took me for millions as well. I feel your pain!"

"Where is the money now?" Arboron demanded, hitting the desk again.

"These charlatans have hidden it all away somewhere. If you find it, please let me know, because I would like to get all of my money back as well."

"What can we do then? We can't just sit here and do nothing!" Arboron shouted, pacing back and forth.

"Law enforcement is dealing with it now. I'm sure if anyone can get to the bottom of this it is the Babbelarian police department. We will just have to wait until they do their job. I'm sure you'll get your money back eventually."

"Eventually? Eventually? I need that capital right now!"

"So sorry, my friend, it's going to take some time," Capitalo said with a condescending smirk. He had paid off the police officers in charge of investigating the case. He knew they were never going to even begin to look into it since they had taken many bribes from him in the past.

Arboron screamed in rage and pounded on the desk again, but Capitalo was unfazed by the threat.

"By the way, it looks like you're bleeding a little bit from your head," Capitalo said with mock concern, waving his hand over his own forehead. "You might want to get someone to take a look at that!"

Arboron picked up one of the chairs in front of Capitalo's desk and threw it across the room. Then he stormed out and marched back to his office in the building next door.

Capitalo smiled a sinister smile. So did the large toad sitting under his large desk.

boi

yeet

CHAPTER 6

The Northern Flight

Loremaster Ebesian never really liked to travel, especially by windship. "We were never meant to fly through the air like birds," he would always say when getting onboard. "It's unnatural." But he did it anyway, because he had to do it.

Tasca put her arm around her grandfather and gave him a hug, knowing it would force him out of his foul mood. "We will soon be there," she whispered.

"Was Aunt Elaine upset that you are joining us on our little adventure?" Ebesian asked her. "I hope she understood why you were asking for a leave of absence."

"No, she wasn't upset. She was excited for me, and I promised that I would help her at the orphanage while we are in Sugstal."

Ebesian's stern expression faded away, and he smiled at her. She was precious to him, so he could not continue to be grumpy. She also reminded him so much of his departed wife. They had the same blonde hair and violet eyes, the same feisty temperament and hearty laugh, and the same way of evoking deep compassion from the depths of his heart.

He put his hands into the pockets of his overcoat because they felt cold. There in his right pocket, his hand touched the simple puzzle box he always carried with him to remind him of his mission.

"When we arrive, I will finally fulfill my destiny," he said with a confidence that made her feel sad and joyful at the same time. She did not like hearing her grandfather talk about completing his life's work. What would happen to him when it was finished? Why were loremasters always so grim?

Ebesian and his students flew northward over the Spygren Fjord. They glided through a narrow ravine with sheer granite cliffs rising up for hundreds of feet on their east and west. The cliffs plunged straight down into the waters of the fjord below for hundreds of feet more. As the morning light fell upon the small village of Sugstal, the Light of Spysar shone brightly in the north, high up in its tower at the southern edge of Lawson's Wood. This lighthouse, and all the other lighthouses throughout Varden, were lit as navigational aids for windships. After the Enemy extinguished the seven beacons, shrouding most of Varden in almost continual darkness, the lighthouses became symbols of hope in a dark, cold world. The first of the seven to be put out was the Beacon of Lisendore. It had been extinguished now for millennia, leaving all of the Eastlands in cold, dark night. That is why Lisendore and the lands to the east were called the Darklands.

The windship landed on the water and coasted to the foot of the Sugstal cliffs. The crew tied it to the docks, and the captain told Ebesian that they had arrived. He quickly packed his books into his bag, slung his sword over his shoulder, and went up on deck. His students were all there, chatting and laughing, smiling and energetic, excited about a new, mysterious adventure. "If only I had so much enthusiasm," Ebesian groaned under his breath as he looked at them and dropped his bags on the deck. His back ached, and he felt as if he had not slept in ages, but he bit his tongue and tried to smile in front of his students anyway. It was the smile of a weary, old man. He felt as dried up and frazzled as his long gray beard.

All of the members of Ebesian's group were handpicked by him personally for this adventure. In addition to his granddaughter, Tasca, daughter of Benton of the royal house of Saren, there were five others.

Mandar, Ebesian's oldest and closest friend, was chosen for his wisdom. The young students had already begun referring to him as "the old man" to his face, and he did not seem to mind. He proudly told them, "I have the gray beard to prove it!" Mandar was the kind of man who was always smiling and jovial. The students enjoyed being around him, and they deeply respected him even when they teased him, which was very often.

Jon was chosen for his courage and strength. He had a muscular build and dark hair that hung down into bright blue eyes. His father, Gathes, was the head of the High Council, and Jon appeared to be following closely in his father's footsteps. He was recognized by the other students as the natural leader of their group because of his out-going, expressive personality.

Traven, son of Zendel, had a thorough knowledge of the Lore. His father also served on the High Council as the Director of Teaching. He had short, light brown hair, blue-green eyes, and a square face. Traven would tell people what he thought they should do, even when they were not asking. The others did not seem to mind though, because he was very often right, especially when it involved a question about the Lore.

Landron stood out in a crowd, because he had a thick mop of curly red hair, sky-blue eyes, and a long, lanky body. He was chosen by Ebesian for his intelligence and his two doctorates in the physical sciences. Everything Landron did had to make logical sense and be right. Often, this trait would annoy the others in the group, but they knew that as long as Landron was around, he would prevent them from making a big mistake.

Gransen had the gift of healing. He had dark brown hair, eyes the color of jade, and a short stocky frame. Gransen cared deeply about others, and was known as a quiet, loyal friend. If someone needed help with a problem, Gransen was the one they confided in.

Ebesian, Mandar, and all of Ebesian's students had been set free from the chains that most of the inhabitants of Varden bear. The chains were once attached to both of their wrists, but now their chains were gone. This happened when each of them chose to pledge their trust and full allegiance to King Tavon. In place of the shack-les, each of the students had silver bands on their wrists, inscribed with ancient runes. Translated into our tongue, the one band read, "Servant of the Highest One." The other band read, "Citizen of Ehadreon—The Eternal City." When they lost their chains, they were also given a special sword from Tavon that they used to fight the nekron. The students, and all those loyal to King Tavon, always carried these swords with them, usually in a scabbard on their backs so that the hilt would be seen above the shoulder.

Gwynneth, of the royal house of Payton, also stowed away onboard the windship. Although she was not invited, being the very definition of a spoiled princess, she insisted on going anyway. She was a silly, plain-looking girl who should have stayed home socializing with aristocrats. She was dressed in a striped orange and green dress that brought out the orange of her eyes and emphasized her vacuous expression. The dress hid an orange and green chain bound to each of her wrists. Ebesian was looking to send her home as soon as possible.

Mandar, all five of the young students, and Gwynneth walked over a gangplank onto the dock. Ebesian waited until they all crossed over. Then he lifted his heavy bags of books and clothes and followed them with a low groan. A grim look had again taken over his face.

Waiting on the docks were Ansen and his two sons. Ansen gave Nathan a nudge and shook his head in Ebesian's direction. Nathan understood what his father meant, so he ran onto the gangplank when Ebesian was about to cross. "I can carry your bag if you would like, Professor," he said.

Ebesian made an effort to smile and said, "Thank you, my boy. That would be kind of you."

Nathan lifted the bags and scurried across the plank to shore. Ebesian followed him, and he noticed they all stood on the dock watching him. He realized they were waiting for further instructions. He tried to straighten his wrinkled robes and overcoat before he gave them the speech he had prepared.

"As you all know, I have sought to serve High King Tavon almost all my life," he said in a loud voice so they all could hear. He was now teaching them, and he felt the grimness beginning to lift from his spirit. "I have learned from him that although life is hard in this cold, dark world, we have the joy of knowing that he will one day return to his rightful throne and restore all things." He put his hand into his pocket and touched the puzzle box. "But until that day comes we have much work to do. The Enemy never rests. The wretched lizards constantly roam back and forth across Varden seeking to devour all that is good. They use their powers of enticement and the misuse of the seven keys to enslave and destroy the people of this world. Every day, the Darklands expand further into the west. We cannot allow this to continue. Now is the time for those of us who are loyal to King Tavon to take a stand against the forces of darkness! He has called upon us to embark upon a very important mission." He paused for a long moment for dramatic effect and then continued, "Today we begin our search for the seven keys to rekindle the beacons of Varden!"

The students were shocked, and there was a collective gasp from the group. Then Jon started shouting, "Yes! Yes!" and he danced around in excitement. Gransen hugged Tasca, Landron looked puzzled, and Traven was smiling broadly. They had studied and trained for this mission for years, and now it was exhilarating to know it was actually about to start. Ansen, Ben and Nathan found their mouths drop open in awe. Only Mandar did not look surprised. Instead, he seemed to have a quiet confidence about him. Ebesian had many long talks with his old friend about what he planned to do. Mandar was relieved to see they were finally taking action after all these years and doing more than just talking.

Gwynneth began smiling broadly and shaking her fists back and forth like a little child about to receive candy. "Oh, this is so exciting," she shouted. "I'm so honored to be a part of this adventure, Master Ebesian!" He looked at her with a very stern expression, but she did not seem notice it. The loremaster sighed and rolled his eyes. Why was this foolish girl bothering him at the beginning of such an important mission?

"Questions," he said in a flat tone as he looked back at his students. He was using his standard method of teaching now, and all the students understood the procedure. He wanted them to show they completely understood what he said, and if they did not understand it, to ask questions until it was crystal clear in their minds. Now he gave them permission to say what they were thinking.

"Professor, are you saying that we are going to try to find not just one or two, but *all seven* of the keys of Ehadreon?" Jon asked.

"Yes," Ebesian said firmly, "all seven." The students were all amazed and smiling at each other.

"But do we even know where they all *are*?" asked Tasca.

"I know where they are. At least I have a very good idea of where they all are. I have been doing research all of my life in the hope of finding the keys. Let's see if I'm right."

They all stood silent for a moment, smiling and looking at each other, and wondering what this new challenge meant to each of them personally. Then Landron asked what they were all thinking. "Where is the first one, Professor?"

"Right here in Sugstal. Unless the Enemy has persuaded someone to move it. If it has been moved, there will be a trail we can follow to its new location. We will find it!"

CHAPTER 7

The Frogorium Spa

Arboron's wife, Histrionicah, was shopping with two of her friends. Shopping was a national pastime for the people of Corasar, and Histrionicah was an expert at it. She would often go shopping for two or three days straight without stopping. She was well-known throughout all of the shops along Purchase Street in the city of Babbelar. The shop owners loved the way Histrionicah freely spent large amounts of cash, but they found it extremely difficult to deal with her temperamental personality. She always took advantage of the number one law of Babbelarian salesclerks: "The customer is always right!" The problem for the shop owners was that she was often wrong.

As Histrionicah bought baubles in downtown Babbelar, the bulky yellow-green chain that was attached to both of her wrists grew a bit more burdensome. It weighed heavy on her neck, but she thought it was a small price to pay for having everything her eyes desired. Besides, everyone she knew had a similar chain, and they all flaunted them in public. The size of a person's chain became something to brag about since everyone knew that the wealthiest and most powerful Corasarians had the biggest chains. They became a badge of success and distinction. Once, in a moment of weakness, Histrionicah returned a very expensive piece of jewelry because she thought she really did not need it. Her chain actually felt lighter when she got home after bringing the jewelry back to the store. After that, she vowed she would never return any of her purchases ever again.

Histrionicah wore a chartreuse dress with a matching round hat on her head. A large peacock feather stuck out of the hat. Her hair was an odd shade of yellowish green, almost the same color as her dress and the chain across her shoulders. Her body was perfectly round, like a ball. If she fell over, she looked like she would just roll right back onto her feet again without missing a beat. Her gaudy makeup made her look like a hideous circus clown. The cosmetics exaggerated her unattractive features, making her large nose look even larger and small chin look even smaller. In her arms, she coddled a rather large frog. A manservant followed her with a cart that was loaded down with boxes. Histrionicah's two friends, Pleonexia and Avarusa, looked like identical copies of her. It was actually very difficult to tell the three of them apart.

"What's the name of your new lap-frog, Histrionicah?" Pleonexia asked.

"I call her Lilypad," Histrionicah answered in her usual nasal tone. "But I often shorten it to Lily when she looks as cute as she does right now!"

"She does look cute, doesn't she?" Avarusa said. Right at that moment, the frog was pursing its lips. "Aww, look, the little froggy wants a kiss!"

Histrionicah held the frog in one hand and poked its belly with the other hand. "Does Lily want a kiss?" she asked as if she was talking to a baby. "Does she? Does she?" The frog looked like it nodded its head, still pursing its lips together. Then she bent over and kissed the frog on the mouth. It was a long, wet kiss, and when it ended, a thick string of mucus extended between Histrionicah's mouth and that of the frog. Avarusa turned away in disgust. Pleonexia laughed out loud.

"I bet she's a better kisser than your husband!" Pleonexia chuckled.

"At least I have a husband!" Histrionicah hissed. "You're so pathetic you'll die a poor, lonely spinster!"

Pleonexia's face flushed with anger, and she turned on her heels and stormed away down Purchase Street without looking back.

"I guess I need to go, too," Avarusa said in a huff. Then she turned and ran after Pleonexia.

"We don't need them anyway, do we Lily?" Histrionicah said to the frog. The frog looked like it shook its head. "Why don't we pamper ourselves a little bit? Would you like that, Lily?" The frog nodded eagerly.

Histrionicah marched down the street to a shop called The Frogorium. She was going to drop Lilypad off at the frog spa. As she walked in, the woman behind the front counter recognized her immediately.

"Good day, Lady Histrionicah. What can we do for you and your wonderful pet today?" the saleswoman asked.

"Lily and I just had quite a shock! I think we need a warm bath and a massage," Histrionicah replied. "And maybe a little swim in the pond first."

"Yes, ma'am. Anything else?" The woman took the frog out of Histrionicah's arms and lifted it over the counter.

"No, I think that's all. I'll be back in about an hour or so."

"Okay, we'll take good care of Lily for you." The saleswoman placed a tag on the frog's leg with a number on it, and she wrote down Histrionicah's name and the number in a logbook. Then she placed the frog on a conveyor belt, and it was whisked into the back room. Histrionicah waved goodbye to the frog and marched out of The Frogorium.

In the back room, a man with an apron and large rubber gloves lifted Lily the frog off the conveyor belt. He dunked it in a vat of water and sprayed it with a few puffs of perfume. Then he placed it in a large cage with ten other frogs and locked the cage door.

"Hey, guys! Look who it is. It's Nefario!" one frog in the cage announced to the others. All the frogs gathered around the newcomer.

"Are you *the* Nefario?" a second frog croaked.

"Yes, I am," Lily—actually Nefario—answered.

"You're legendary!" the second frog said. "You're the one who caused the run on the banks five years ago!"

"Yeah, that's me," Nefario said, looking less and less like Lily by the moment.

"What are you doin' now, Nefario?" a third frog asked.

"I'm working to bring down the biggest businessman in Babbelar. A guy by the name of Arboron and his wife, Histrionicah," Nefario answered.

"Arboron! Wow, you're really going after the big fish!" the third frog said.

"The big ones are more fun!" Nefario bragged. All the frogs in the cage croaked in agreement. Nefario looked down and shook his head. "Actually, it's not as much fun as it was in the old days," he croaked. "Now it's like shooting fish in a barrel. In the old days, we used to have to hide and use our wits to tempt our victims. It took real skill to ruin their lives. Now things are so easy. We've made them so greedy they don't even put up a fight. They're so stupid it's not much of a challenge anymore."

"But that means we've been successful!" the first frog suggested. All the other frogs croaked their agreement.

"Yes," Nefario said, "but I liked it when we really had to work for it. These greedy Corasarians are just idiots. They treat us like lovable pets! They don't even realize we're destroying their very souls!"

All the frogs in the cage croaked with fiendish laughter. All of Corasar was completely under their control, and the Corasarians had no idea what was even happening.

CHAPTER 8

The Eternal City

A tall, handsome woodsman suddenly materialized out of thin air near the beautiful garden at the center of Ehadreon—the Eternal City of the Great King. He carried a large sword on his back. As he waved his arms out to the side, his rough woodsman clothing transformed into a bright white uniform. A dazzling, golden glow permeated everything around him—even the glass-like pavement under his feet and the huge fruit trees and amazing flowers that surrounded him. This *engven* was named Anskar. He had been summoned by King Tavon to give a report on his latest assignment. He knew that Tavon must have important plans to share with him, or he would not have been asked to come to the royal throne at the center of the city.

Tavon's throne was an impressive sight. It shone with an eternal radiance that blinded the eyes of those unprepared to see it. A river, clear as crystal, flowed from the throne down the middle of the Great Street of the city. At the head of the river, just behind the throne, stood a huge tree—the Tree of Life. It bore fruit perpetually all throughout the year, and its leaves had amazing healing properties. Anyone who ate from the tree would live forever and never die.

Anskar walked up the Great Street toward the Tree of Life. When he saw the king standing near his throne at the foot of the tree, Anskar knelt down on one knee and bowed his head.

King Tavon was surrounded by a bright, blue light that radiated out from him in all directions. His bright, violet eyes held the wisdom of a million ages. His thick hair and beard were as white as snow. The crown on his head looked like it was made from a branch of a thorn bush that had been twisted together and dipped in gold. He wore a bright blue cape over a brilliant, white uniform with a golden sash across his chest. On the cape, and on the side of his right leg, ancient runes declared his title: "King of All Kings."

The king walked toward his servant and said, "How is your assignment going, Anskar?"

Anskar looked up at Tavon but continued to kneel. "Young Litfim is very active, Your Majesty. Yesterday I saved him from drowning in the fjord. The day before that, I stopped him from jumping off the roof of the orphanage."

Tavon laughed. "That's what I love about Litfim. He's so bold and curious. He's going to do great things for my kingdom!" The king sat down on the throne and smiled brightly.

"That is if we can make sure he does not arrive here in the Eternal City too early, Your Majesty!" Anskar said with a hint of concern in his voice.

"Litfim will have a long and full life on Varden, and you will have the joy of making sure of it."

"Yes, Your Majesty." Anskar knew that Tavon's plans always came to fruition, so he had no doubt that what he was saying was true.

"That is why I asked you to come here today. Litfim is going to explore the ruined mansion south of Sugstal tomorrow. Protect the boy, but do not stop him from going there."

"The mansion, Your Majesty? That place is crawling with enemy worms! Please give me a team of engven to clear it out before the boy goes there."

"No, I don't want to alert the enemy to the fact that Litfim is doing something very significant for my kingdom. Let them think that a naive orphan boy has stumbled into the wrong place at the wrong time! They will make the mistake of thinking that he is harmless."

"How much of a risk should I allow the boy to take?"

"Protect him from losing his life or his health, but permit him to experience a bit of fear and hardship. Litfim is going to discover what it means to be courageous for me tomorrow. It will prepare him for what I have in store for him in the future." Tavon stood up from the throne. "Do not allow yourself to be seen inside the mansion by friend or foe, and do not engage the enemy unless you are absolutely sure the boy's life is at stake. I don't want the enemy to know Litfim is important or that what he is about to do will forever change the history of Varden for the better."

"Yes, Your Majesty." Anskar bowed his head again. "I serve only to please you, my Lord and King."

King Tavon stepped over to Anskar and placed his hands on Anskar's shoulders to bless him. There were scars on both of Tavon's hands—the scars from his greatest battle. The king took Anskar's sword in his hand and it shone with a blinding, white light, more brilliant than the sun. Anskar tried to shield his eyes from the dazzling radiance. "Go in my name! Your success is guaranteed, Anskar!"

"Thank you, my king."

Tavon placed the sword back in Anskar's hands. Anskar bowed his head once more and stood to his feet. He bowed again and slowly backed away from the king. Only when he could no longer see Tavon did he turn his back toward the throne. He waved his arms out to the side and his white uniform changed back into his woodsman clothing. Then he ran down the Great Street of the city, away from the immense Tree of Life. When he reached his top speed, he dematerialized in a flash of light.

CHAPTER 9

The Orphan's Adventure

A young orphan wandered throughout the village of Sugstal just before noontime. Everyone called him Litfim, which in the Ancient Tongue meant "little man." He was nine years old, with a mop of blonde hair and bright blue eyes. He was clean but poorly dressed, small but strong. He should have been in school, but he was bored and restless. He was looking for something more exciting to do than memorizing multiplication tables. He also knew that the gatekeeper at the southern end of the village always liked to go to the *White Stallion* for their meat pies around this time of the day. It would be easier for him to sneak out the southern gate if no one asked him a lot of questions.

Since he was smart and very friendly by nature, he had learned how to persuade others to be generous. Today, he managed to convince the baker and the grocer to give him some lunch. *It was pretty puny*, he thought. *Only a little cake, a few pieces of bread, and a couple of tiny sardines.* It would have to hold him until he could get back to the orphanage for supper.

He made sure not to draw too much attention to himself as he neared the southern end of the village. When he thought no one was watching, he darted through the South Gate and started walking quickly down the dirt road. There was an old dilapidated mansion about a mile south of Sugstal, just off the South Road. He thought he should go there to explore and eat his meal.

He quietly walked toward the front of the house. *It is quite a large place*, he thought. *It will take hours to explore all of its rooms and passages.* So he decided it would be best to eat before he started his adventure. "I need the energy," he said out loud to himself.

He went up a wide staircase and sat down with his back to the wall in the alcove by the two front doors. As he took his meager lunch out of his pocket, a crazed-looking man came around the corner.

"Who are you? What are you doing here?" the man shouted. His eyes were a sickening shade of yellow green. His thin, stringy hair stuck out in all directions from a balding scalp. A heavy green chain was wrapped around his neck and attached to his wrists. His body was thin and wiry. His once expensive clothes were torn and filthy. He seemed to be so nervous and jittery that it was impossible for him to stay still.

"My name is Litfim. I just wanted to sit and eat my lunch." Litfim was frightened by the man because he looked like someone who was capable of acting on whatever came into his twisted mind.

"Gimme that!" the man shouted. He grabbed Litfim's food and began stuffing it into his mouth all at once. He mumbled something while he was eating, but it was hard for Litfim to understand him when his mouth was full.

"If you're hungry, sir, I would have gladly shared my lunch with you," Litfim said meekly.

"Share! Share?" The man held what was left of the bread in his hand, and he pointed it at Litfim. "This is mine. Do you understand? I wished for it. It's all mine!" he said, spitting out his words and bits of sardines. "Why would I *share* it with *you*?" He turned away from the boy and swallowed the rest of the bread.

"King Tavon has always given me all I need. I never go hungry. He can help you as well if you'd let him," Litfim said as he slowly stood up, watching the man very carefully.

"I serve no king!" the man shouted, turning back around. "I am my *own* king! The master of my own fate! I am no one's slave!" He felt the chain around his throat tighten and pull him backwards a bit. He pulled it forwards so that he found it easier to breathe.

38

Litfim knew at once the man was insane. But how do you handle a crazy person? They never taught him anything in school about talking to someone who is totally mad. He realized the best thing to do was run. *Hopefully the lunatic is so starved he will not be able to keep up with me*, he thought.

As the man shoved the pastry into his mouth, Litfim moved like a flash. He flew down the steps and around toward the northern side of the house. The man ran after him, but he began choking, so he stopped and bent over as he started coughing. Litfim kept running as fast as he could along the side of the mansion when he suddenly saw a large wall in front of him. He looked back over his left shoulder. The wall ran parallel to house all the way back to the front doors. He was trapped! He was so eager to escape from the madman that he did not even notice the wall until it was too late.

He heard the man shouting curses at him. He was getting closer. Litfim looked around, and he saw that his only escape was a broken window on the side of the mansion. He jumped up and grabbed hold of the window sill, and then he pulled himself up and through the opening. He fell into the room, but he did not seem to have hurt himself very badly. "All those days climbing trees were worth it," he said to himself.

Litfim found himself in the western end of a large library. Tall bookcases lined all of the walls, but all of the books lay in large piles on the floor. The entire room was filled with heaps of books and a pale green dust. The dust seemed to glow faintly as it hung in the air.

Litfim tried to look for a door, but the piles of books blocked his view of any escape. In the center of the room was a desk filled with stacks of paper. The only light in the room shone from the desk, so he headed toward the light. Maybe he could see where the door was from the middle of the room. He could stand on the desk if he needed to.

When he got to the desk, he noticed a large key had been placed in the center of it, on top of a red stained blotter. The key was the source of the light. It glowed with an unappealing yellow-green color. It also had been twisted out of shape so that it looked mangled and useless. His curiosity made him slowly reach out and touch it. Just a quick little tap. Suddenly the key began to straighten out. Litfim jumped back, but then he got closer again as the key fully untwisted itself. It began to glow with a bright, violet light. He reached out and quickly poked his finger at the key again. To his amazement, it suddenly disappeared.

Just then, the crazed man ran into the southern side of the library, and he saw the boy standing at the desk. Litfim tried to get back to the western window, but he slipped on some books and the man got to that side of the room first. He quickly turned and ran toward the eastern side of the library and hid under a table. He shut his eyes and started praying that the man would not harm him.

"Come on out, little boy," the man whined, as he walked toward the center of the room. "My name is Viridan. I promise I won't hurt you. Look, I saved some of the cake for you."

Actually, he had eaten all the pastry. He had nothing in his green hands but the heavy chain that was also around his neck. Viridan walked past the desk in the middle of the room. As he walked by, he glanced over and he noticed the key was gone! He suddenly flew into a rage.

"I'm going to kill you when I find you!" he ranted. "Where is it, runt? What have you done with it?" He was filled with so much anger that he began knocking over stacks of books and throwing them in all directions.

The madman came close to the table where Litfim was hiding, but he did not look underneath it. He walked past him and began knocking down piles in the eastern end of the room. Litfim came out from under the table and ran back the way he came. The man heard the sound of books dropping and he ran back in the same direction. Litfim realized he had no time to get out of the window, so he sprinted toward the door on the southern side where the man had entered. The man was almost on top of him now, but Litfim pushed over a stack of large volumes in the man's path and they fell on him.

Litfim flew out the door and into a large dining room. He jumped over broken chairs and pottery and out through another set of doors into another room. It was very large and very dark, but he could see light coming through an opening far away at its other side.

40

He kept running toward the light. Soon he was back at the front doors. He jumped down the stairs and onto the path leading to the road. He did not look back as he ran down the pathway—not even when he felt the madman grab his collar. He just stomped hard on the man's foot and kept running when he had broken free of his grasp.

The madman tripped over something and fell on his face as he tried to run after him. Litfim knew that he fell, because he saw him on the ground out of the corner of his eye as he reached the road to Sugstal. He turned around at the end of the pathway to catch his breath, and he saw the man lying on the ground sobbing. Although Litfim felt sorry for him, he decided it was best for someone else to help a madman with his troubles, and he ran off down the South Road as fast as his legs could carry him.

He did not see the large woodsman standing on the pathway between him and the madman. If he had seen him, he would have known that he had nothing to fear.

CHAPTER 10

The Clueless Captain

Ben rolled up a pile of navigation charts. He put them under his arm, and he walked out of the front door of the windship launch office. He turned left on High Street, and he marched directly to the front door of the *White Stallion*. He went inside and sat down at his usual table in the corner by the window. Then he unrolled the charts on the scarred, wooden table, and he began studying them intently.

A beautiful waitress with dark hair, tan skin, and violet eyes came over to his table. Sasha smiled brightly and said, "What can I get for you today, Bensareon?"

"Oh, I'll just have my usual," he said, barely looking up from his charts. "Thanks," he said, looking back down.

Sasha shook her head slightly and pressed her lips together as she turned and walked toward the kitchen. She thought Ben was handsome and intelligent, but he never showed any interest in her. All the other young men flirted with her, but Ben hardly acknowledged her existence. "That's his loss!" she said to herself as she pushed open the door to the kitchen.

Just then, Ebesian's five students came through the front door, all talking and smiling at the same time. They took off their coats, hung their swords on the backs of their chairs, and sat down at a table in the middle of the room. Jon was telling a story, and they were all laughing loudly as they listened to him.

"Then the professor said, 'If you are not going to do something with that, Mister Padren, I suggest you put it back in your pocket!'

The whole class thought it was hysterical." Jon laughed so hard tears ran down his face.

Traven and Gransen were holding their bellies and laughing so hard they were sliding out of their chairs. Tasca was laughing so hard she felt like she could not draw air into her lungs. Even Landron was laughing out loud.

"Oh, I can't breathe," Tasca whispered, fanning her face with her hand. "I need to breathe!"

"That's good!" said Gransen. "Oh, that's funny," he said wiping his eyes with his sleeve.

The five of them sat quietly for a moment trying to regain their composure. Tasca looked at Jon and she felt drawn to him. He was good looking and witty. She had always thought of him as a snobbish brute. Now he appeared to be so much more than that. He seemed heroic somehow.

When Ben heard all the laughter, he looked up from his charts. Who was making such a racket and ruining his concentration? He saw Tasca with the four other students, laughing at a table in the center of the room. He couldn't take his eyes off her smile. He stared at her, thinking that if he looked away, some sort of incredible beauty would vanish from the world and be lost forever. When she looked over in his direction, he self-consciously looked back down at the table. He tried to study the charts in front of him, but he found it hard to concentrate.

Just then, Sasha came back to the table with a plate of shepherd's pie. She placed it on the table, on top of the charts, right under Ben's nose. When he looked up, he saw her leaning over the table very close to him. Her face almost brushed against his cheek. She gave him her brightest, warmest smile, and said, "The usual, shepherd's pie."

He leaned back in his chair because she had come so close to him. In a very matter-of-fact way, he said, "Thanks."

"You're welcome," she said as she turned back toward the kitchen. She looked back at him when she reached the kitchen door. She was hoping that he was still watching her. Instead, he was staring off into the middle of the room. Disappointed, she pushed the kitchen door open and walked back inside.

Ben slowly began to eat his pie. He tried to study the charts in front of him, but he could not focus his eyes on them. They just looked like indistinct lines and meaningless blotches of color. Tasca's smile was the only thing he could think about at the moment. Occasionally, he would take a glance over at Tasca's table. She was surely enjoying the company of the four young men, especially that guy Jon. She was leaning toward him with one hand under her chin and her elbow on the table. She seemed to be enamored with him for some reason.

Ben felt like Nathan was right. A girl like Tasca would never really take an interest in him. *Isn't that the way it is?* Ben thought. *You really like someone, but they don't even know you're alive.*

CHAPTER 11

The Lost Orphan

It was getting very dark now, and Litfim was regretting his decision to go exploring that day. He felt hungry and tired. He had no choice but to continue walking up the road toward home and safety.

As he came around a bend, he saw a gypsy wagon on the side of the road. *I should ask for help*, he thought. He ran up to the wagon. Two men sat up front drinking something from pewter tankards. One was large and hairy with yellow eyes. He did not strike Litfim as being very intelligent. The other was more muscular and had a close-cropped beard. He had red eyes, a long scar down the left side of his face, and a mean expression. Litfim thought he seemed to be the smarter of the two.

"Sir, can you help me? I need to get back to the village," he said to the smarter looking one.

"Sure, my lad, that's no problem. We're heading in that direction anyway." The man said the right words, but something was wrong with his expression. Litfim did not trust him, but he climbed up into the wagon anyway. He had to get home.

Litfim sat between the two men as the wagon moved on down the road. They sat in silence as the horses slowly pulled the large wagon northward. He soon discovered that the hairier man had a really bad odor. He also learned the more intelligent looking man was called Stang. He was hoping the trip would not last very long.

After a little while, Stang said, "You hungry, boy?"

"No," he said. Actually, the rancid odor of the man next to him was making him nauseous. "I'm just a little thirsty."

Stang took a flask out of his coat and poured some liquid into one of the tankards. "Here lad, drink this. It'll make you feel better."

Litfim took the tankard in both hands and cautiously sipped at the liquid. It tasted pleasant and quite sweet. He drank down the rest and he began to feel very groggy. Soon he fell fast asleep.

* * * * *

On the northern edge of Sugstal, close to the western end of the narrow Bergendore Fjord, there was an orphanage. The Daughters of Compassion started it about twenty years earlier with the approval of the High Council. The children there were treated with kindness, they were well fed and clothed, and they were thoroughly instructed in the Lore, as well as reading, writing, mathematics, and history. Lady Elaine ran the orphanage with a firm yet loving hand. Years ago, she gave up the great wealth and privilege of the royal house of Saren to build the orphanage. The children adored her, and the other Daughters did not dare to challenge her authority.

In spite of all the love and kindness the Daughters displayed to the orphans, a few still got into trouble from time to time. One of them, young Litfim, seemed to get into trouble all the time. He was a free spirit, as they say, and the Daughters were used to having to ask men from the village to find him when he wandered off. This day, the staff had searched all over the orphanage grounds and they still could not find him, so Lady Elaine asked Ben and Nathan to look for him.

"Litfim has been missing all day!" she said. "I'm really worried this time. It's getting dark. He usually gets hungry and finds his way back home by suppertime!"

"Don't worry, we'll find him. He's probably in the woods climbing trees, or building a castle or something," Nathan replied.

Nathan and Ben began looking in all the usual places. First, they went to the redwood forest north of the orphanage, but Litfim was not there. Then they went back into the village and began asking people in the *White Stallion* if they had seen the boy. No one there had seen him all day.

Sasha, who was waiting on tables at the *White Stallion*, noticed Ben and Nathan asking all the customers questions. "Hi, Nathan. Hi, Bensareon. What's the matter?"

"A boy named Litfim is missing from the orphanage," Ben said with a serious expression. "Have you seen him?"

"Yes, he came to the back door just before lunchtime looking for food," Sasha said. "I usually give him something, but I knew that he was supposed to be in school. So I told him that he needed to get back to class or he would be in big trouble."

"Which way did he go when he left here?" Nathan asked.

"I thought he listened to me and headed back toward the orphanage."

"Lady Elaine and the staff haven't seen him all day."

"Litfim does this all the time," Sasha said, shaking her head. "He's probably sitting in the back of one of the village shops eating sweets!"

"I hope so! Please let us know if you see him."

Ben and Nathan left the *White Stallion* and started walking south on High Street. "Now there's a girl I would really like to spend more time with," Nathan said to his brother.

"What girl?" Ben asked.

"Sasha! She's beautiful, intelligent and really cares about people. I see her down at the orphanage helping out all the time. She even brings food to the old gypsies."

"She looks like she might be a gypsy herself."

"She is. She lives in a wagon just south of the village. What's wrong with being a gypsy?"

"Nothing! I just don't understand how you know so much about her."

"Because, unlike my hermit of a brother, I actually talk to people and get to know them. Especially if they're attractive young women. You should try it some time. Maybe you wouldn't be so lonely."

"Nathan, where did you speak to Sasha? It's not like you spend a lot of time around the gypsy wagons."

"At the prayerhouse here in the village. She's there every week on the Day of Resting."

"I never noticed her there."

"Open your eyes, brother!"

Ben and Nathan continued down High Street asking the shop owners if they had seen Litfim. The baker said he gave him a pastry, but he did not see which way he went when he left his shop. They headed further south on High Street, checking with all the shops as they went along. The grocer told them he gave him some bread and a few sardines and that he headed down toward the southern shops. After questioning everyone they saw, they began to think he might have left the village through the South Gate.

"What are we going to do?" Ben asked his brother.

"Let's go back and get help. Maybe Ebus and his students can help us find him."

They walked back to the *Wayside Inn* in the center of the village, where Ebesian and his students were staying. "You don't think this has anything to do with that key Ebus mentioned, do you?" Ben asked Nathan as they entered the inn.

"No, don't be daft! But maybe that will be a good reason for them to help us find Litfim."

Ben felt deep down that the fate of little Litfim and the key were all bound together, but he did not try to explain it to his brother, because he did not even know how to explain it to himself.

CHAPTER 12

The Poor Benefactor

Viridan sat on the floor of his ruined mansion mumbling to himself. Although he was about the same age as Ebesian's twenty-year-old students, he appeared to be older than Ebesian himself. Green and yellow dust covered everything around him, especially his hands. He lay weeping and rubbing his hands together in an attempt to remove the yellow-green stain on them, but it was to no avail. He gave up trying to wipe them off, and he pounded them on the marble floor instead. Then he screamed out in pain and fell forward on to his face. He lay sprawled on the floor, sobbing because he had broken his hand.

He eventually stood up and limped over a large chandelier that had crashed to the ground. A heavy green chain dragged behind him. He pulled it up and threw it over his shoulder, and then he continued to stagger forward. He wandered from the large stone foyer, with its wide double staircases, into the darkness of the marbled great hall with its tattered curtains and stained tapestries. He went on into the wood-paneled dining room. The ceiling had collapsed here, and its rubble lay on top of the large, mahogany table in the center of the room. Once ornate chairs and fine china lie broken on the floor. The stained-glass windows were cracked and pieces were missing in places, so he could easily see outside. He walked up to the window and peered out into what was once a verdant garden, but what was now a brown and lifeless patch of weeds. He wanted to know if his "guest" was still there, so he climbed through the broken window and stepped out into the courtyard.

Out by a leafless tree, in the middle of the garden, was a large snake, at least ten feet long and eight inches wide. It had tiny, little, useless legs sticking out from its side, and a large, black chain wrapped around its body. It coiled itself around the branches of the tree, and it slowly turned its head to look directly at Viridan. Then it opened its mouth wide, baring two large fangs.

Fear of the snake made Viridan's spine tingle, and he began to cry and shake. "No-oo!" he shouted. "Leave me alone! What do I have to do to be *rid* of you?"

"You gladly welcomed me into your home," hissed the snake. "I gave you the key to great wealth. I gave you all you asked for. Why would you want to be rid of your benefactor?"

"You said I would be happy, but I'm far from happy! I'm miserable!" Viridan shouted holding his head.

"So use my gift to create more for yourself," the snake said in a soothing voice as it slid down the tree. "You'll feel better if you have more. Just make a wish and you will have everything you desire."

"It's been stolen. That little thief took it from me," Viridan cried.

"Don't worry. You still have all of your beautiful things," the snake said, as it slowly slithered closer to the mansion.

"What 'things?' I have no '*things*!'" shouted Viridan. He turned around to look back on all his broken possessions. "Look! They're all garbage now! It's all worthless! Totally worthless!"

"So are you!" declared the snake, and with a lunge, it swallowed Viridan whole.

CHAPTER 13

The Orphan's Interrogation

The gypsies had circled their wagons in a clearing in the woods about two miles from the South Road to Sugstal. Stang held a large, yellow-green key in his black-gloved hand. It was twisted out of shape and faintly glowing. During the night, they had searched through Litfim's clothes and found it in his coat pocket. They knew it was unusual because it changed from violet to green when they touched it. It also looked straight at first, but now it was mangled. They thought it must be something magical.

"Where did you get this, boy?" Stang growled.

Litfim sat on a lopsided stool. He trembled as the huge man towered over him. They had taken him into the back of a covered gypsy wagon to interrogate him. That morning, he woke up with a terrible headache made all the worse by Stang's shouting at him.

"It's from that big house near the South Road. The one that's falling down." The boy's voice squeaked and broke as he spoke. He seemed so tiny in the shadow of Stang's six-and-a-half-foot bulk. He felt small and frail, his courage and curiosity gone.

"What does it open?" Stang asked.

"I don't know. I don't even know how it got here."

"It was in *your* pocket. Don't lie to me, boy!" Stang shouted.

"I'm not lying! When I touched it, it changed and then it disappeared!"

"And it landed in *your* pocket!" Stang shouted in the boy's face.

"Yes, I guess so," he said meekly, but Stang was clearly not satisfied with his answers.

"Tell me the truth!" Stang growled as he took the boy by the throat.

Litfim began to pray. He had to say the right thing to convince Stang of his honesty. Stang was looking for the whole story. He had to prove he was telling the truth. Then the words came to him. He said them all as fast as he could.

"I went to this wrecked house. I thought no one was there, but a crazy man chased me. I ran away, but there was a wall, so I ran into the house. I saw the key on the desk. It changed colors and disappeared. The man chased me and I ran away. I walked down the road and saw you." *There, the whole story, the whole truth*, he thought.

Stang relaxed his grip on the boy's neck a little and said, "When was the first time you saw the key?"

"Yesterday," the boy said, tears filling his eyes.

"Are you lying to me?"

"No, yesterday, I swear."

Stang studied the boy closely for a moment, and then he let him go. He could tell when someone was lying to him, because he was an expert liar. This boy seemed to be telling him the truth.

"We want you to show us where you found it, okay?"

The boy nodded his head timidly. The hairy, smelly man grabbed his arm and pulled him back out of the wagon. The man's hand had a large yellow-green stain on it now. Litfim hoped that he did not contaminate him or his clothes with it.

Stang, the smelly man, and another man with an eye patch put Litfim into an open wagon, and they went back to where they found him the night before on the South Road.

"Where is the house?" Stang asked him.

"Just a little ways farther down the road."

When they got to the pathway leading to the mansion, Litfim told them to stop, and they all got out of the wagon.

"Go ahead, lad. Show us where it is," Stang commanded.

The last place Litfim wanted to go was back to the madman's house, but the three huge men with red scarves tied around their massive heads were more intimidating to him right now than the lunatic, so he began walking toward the house. *Maybe when they start fighting the crazy man I can escape*, he thought.

"No runnin' off now, boy," the smelly one said. "We wouldn't want ta have to catch ya. It'd make us very cross."

"And you don't want us cross," said the other man with a black eye patch over one eye. "When we is cross we gets hungry, and our favorite meal is little boy's liver!"

The two men laughed. Stang came up behind the eye patch man and hit him sharply on the back of the head with a short club. He whispered, "Don't scare him, you idiot. We want him to show us where he found it. There may be other valuables there."

They continued walking until they came to the front of Viridan's dilapidated mansion. Litfim pointed to it and said, "In there."

"Good, show us exactly where it was," Stang said in a deep, soothing voice.

The three men followed Litfim through the double front doors and into the formerly grand foyer. Yellow-green dust covered furniture that was gray and tattered. They continued walking through the great hall, and the sound of their footsteps echoed off the marble walls. Litfim slowly stuck his head through the open door to the dining room. It was darker than he remembered. The men brushed past him and went inside. They split up and began examining things separately. The smelly man soon shouted, "Hey boss, look at this!"

Stang and the man with the eye patch ran over to the spot. The skeleton of a man lay on the floor. It was a strange, bright green color. The bones looked slimy and they were still connected to each other by ligaments and tissue. "This happened recently," Stang whispered. "It's best we don't stay here too long," he said, drawing out a large knife. "There's nothing of worth here anyway."

Litfim did not walk over toward the skeleton. Instead he walked over to a side door. "I found it in here," he said to the men.

They followed him into a library filled with books that had fallen from the tall shelves on every wall. They lay in huge piles near the bookcases. Stang picked one up. The title was *Dream Your Way to Financial Happiness*. He tossed it aside and picked up another.

It read *Building Larger Storage Barns.* Another said, *Claiming Your Substantial Fortune.* "Guess that didn't work for the pile of bones out there," Stang said to himself as he tossed the book back onto the pile.

Litfim led them to a desk in the middle of the room. Large piles of paper cluttered its surface. A large, red ink stain covered the blotter in the center. "I found it there," Litfim said, pointing at the desk.

Stang looked over the pages on the desk. There were overdue bills from various merchants, a letter from a bank threatening to foreclose on some property, IOU notes from gambling debts, and blackmail threats from a woman demanding more money. Stang opened all of the drawers. All he saw was more of the same kind of papers that were on the top of the desk. "Nothing of value here," Stang said to his men. "You sure this is it, boy?" he said looking down on Litfim.

"Yes, sir," the boy said quietly. He suddenly found it was hard to swallow. He began trembling again. Sweat started flowing down his face. What would they do with him now?

"Okay, let's go then," Stang commanded his men.

The three of them walked out of the room, leaving little Litfim standing there all alone. The boy stood still for a long time. He did not move because he was just so afraid. He thought they would come back and drag him out of the room, but they did not. He could not believe they were really gone.

He slowly began walking back through the house. When he reached the foyer, he peeked out the front doors to see if his captors were gone. He heard them talking and laughing as they began walking down the road back toward their wagon.

He sat down outside the house, hiding in the bushes. He decided to wait until he was really certain the coast was clear. As the fear began to drain from his small body, he became very tired and he fell asleep.

"I smell someone in league with the Enemy," hissed the snake from the garden courtyard. Its forked tongue darted in and out. It seemed to have grown larger in the last day. Looking down from a tree high above the front of the mansion it said, "Ahh, I see him. A scrawny, little snack. Yet he will do for my dessert."

The snake eased himself down from the tree. The heavy chain around his body snagged on a branch for a moment, but he managed to pull it free, and he dropped onto the ground. Even though he had tiny, little legs sticking out from his side, the snake slithered on his belly toward a slumbering Litfim. As he began to unhinge his jaw to swallow the boy, he suddenly felt intense agony. He turned his head and saw a large woodsman standing over him with a bright sword.

"Engven! Curses! Curses on all your ..." it said, as the woodsman easily lopped off its head. The snake vanished in a cloud of dark smoke.

"What are you doing here, little one?" the woodsman whispered as he lifted the boy. "You sure keep me busy." He brushed the boy's hair aside to see if he was all right.

"Hi, Anskar. How are you?" Litfim said to the woodsman holding him.

"I'm fine, but you are not. You have to stay inside the village walls. Is that clear?"

"Yes, sir."

Anskar put him down. "You've promised me you wouldn't leave Sugstal a hundred times now. Have you learned your lesson?"

"Yes, sir," the boy said meekly. He was ashamed that Anskar was scolding him again, but it also made him feel important somehow.

"One day, I might not be there to protect you. Now head on home. You'll see two men from the village on the road. They're looking for you. They will get you home safely."

Litfim started walking toward the road to Sugstal. He turned around and smiled at Anskar and said, "Thanks again. Sorry!"

He turned on to the South Road, and he immediately saw Ben and Landron walking toward him. They both ran to him. "Where have you been, Litfim? We were looking everywhere for you. Lady Elaine is worried sick about you," Ben said.

As Ben knelt down by the boy, he saw a figure standing in the distance behind him. He looked very familiar. Yet as soon as Ben focused his attention on the man, he seemed to fade into the background. The three of them started walking back toward the village, but Ben could not shake the idea that he had seen that man many times before. He kept looking over his shoulder on the way home. He felt that he might gain a glimpse of the woodsman again if the light was just right.

CHAPTER 14

The Yellow-Green Stain

The big, hairy man sat all alone on a chair in the gypsy camp, talking to himself and rubbing his hand. His thick, untamed, black beard covered much of his pockmarked face. Long, black hair stuck out from under a colorful scarf on his large head. No one usually ate with Berk, because he did not wash very often and he smelled quite awful.

He got up and poured some water on the yellow-green stain on his right hand and rubbed it, but it did not seem to do much good. He even tried to wash it with soap, which was something he rarely used. The stain did not seem to fade. It appeared to be permanently burned into his skin.

A lizard, about two feet long, scurried across the ground. It came out of the woods and lay down right under Berk's chair. The black chain around its neck was also attached to the two legs on its right side. Those two legs appeared to be stunted.

The lizard whispered, "I wish I could see that key again."

"I wish I could see that key again," Berk mumbled to himself. "Stang said that the key must be very important. It's probably magical."

"Wish I could just take a peek at it," said the lizard.

"Wish I could just peek at it," Berk said.

Suddenly, Stang stepped down out of his gypsy wagon, and he walked toward a group of people eating at the other end of the camp.

"This is my chance to see it," whispered the lizard.

"This is my chance to see it," repeated Berk.

Berk stood up and tiptoed over to Stang's wagon. He carefully looked around to make sure he was not seen, and he quietly opened the door to the wagon and went inside. As he opened the door the lizard slipped in unnoticed by Berk.

"Now where would it be?" asked the lizard.

"Now where would it be?" mumbled Berk.

He began looking under the bed and the mattress. Then he searched a desk in the corner by the door. Not finding the key, he moved on to the dresser. On top of the dresser he found a pair of black leather gloves. They had a greenish powder on them. He opened the top drawer and searched through the clothing there. In the back of the drawer, he found a sack with a drawstring on the top. He could feel something large and hard was inside the sack. Opening it up, he found the key. It was glowing with a yellow-green hue, and it was twisted out of shape. When he found it in the boy's pocket, it was not bent and it was glowing violet, but as soon as he touched the key, it warped and changed to its present color.

"It's magical," said the lizard. "I should take it."

"It's magic," Berk said. "I'll take it!"

Berk put the key back in the sack and put it in his coat pocket. Then he quietly opened the door and tiptoed down the steps. He turned to his left and ran off into the woods to look at his prize in secret. The lizard scurried along behind him.

He was afraid that Stang would know that he stole the key, so he ran all the way back to the South Road. He sat down in the woods on a hill overlooking the road and took the key out of his pocket. The lizard crawled up beside him, but he did not see it. Berk rubbed the key gently.

"How I can get its magic to work?" asked the lizard.

How does its magic work? thought Berk.

"Maybe it grants wishes," the lizard said.

"Maybe it grants wishes," Berk repeated.

"Now what should I wish for?" asked the lizard.

"What should I wish for?" Berk asked out loud.

At first, he could not think of anything. Then he realized that he had not eaten any supper. He was hungry. "I know," he said. He closed his eyes tightly, rubbed the key, and said, "I wish I had a feast!" Then he opened his eyes. A look of disappointment fell over his face when he did not immediately see any food in front of him. "I guess it doesn't work!" he declared.

"It works, it works," the lizard hissed as it scurried off into the woods besides the road.

After about five minutes a covered wagon appeared around the bend in the road. A young man named Trine drove a wagon pulled by two tired, old horses. He was a kind-hearted shopkeeper who ran a small grocery on High Street in Sugstal.

Berk did not read very well, but he could see from the meats, fruits, and vegetables painted on its side that it was a grocer's wagon. "Ha, ha!" he said out loud as he saw the wagon. He stood up and shouted, "It works, it works!"

The wagon continued slowly down the road until it was close to where Berk was standing on the hill. Suddenly he heard a loud crack, and a large branch fell off a tree and onto the road. Clinging to the branch was the lizard.

The branch now blocked the path of the wagon, so Trine quickly reined in the horses and brought it to a stop. He jumped down from the wagon to look at the obstacle in his way. Then he went inside the wagon. A moment later, he came out with an ax in his hand. He sighed loudly and started chopping at the branch. It was going to take him a long time to cut it up and move it away. Trine was a tall man, but he was not very strong. The ax was also very dull.

"It works," Berk whispered, "but how am I goin' to git the food? I know." Berk closed his eyes and rubbed the key again saying, "I wish I was invisible. I wish I was invisible." When Berk opened his eyes, he looked down at his hands and they were gone! The key seemed to be floating in midair. He looked for his feet and legs and they were gone, too! He felt like his body was still there, but now he was completely invisible. He put the key in his pocket. "Ha, ha! It works! It works!" he shouted, as he ran down the hill toward the wagon.

When Trine heard the shouting, he stopped cutting the branch and looked up. He saw a large, hairy gypsy running toward the back of his wagon. "Hey, what are you doing?" the grocer shouted at him. He thought the gypsies must have cut down the branch in order to stop the wagon and rob him. As he came around to the back of the wagon, he saw that the gypsy had opened the back doors. The brute was looking inside and about to grab a large turkey. "Stop what you are doing, right now!" Trine commanded.

Berk lifted the turkey out of the wagon. "Ha, ha!" he laughed, as the turkey appeared to float out of the back of the wagon. "Try to stop an invisible man!"

Trine looked confused, and he shook his head. "Who's invisible? I can see you!"

But Berk heard his words differently. He thought he heard the grocer say, "Who is invisible? I can't see you!"

Berk ran over to the side of the road and dropped the turkey in the snow. Then he tiptoed back and lifted a large basket of vegetables out of the wagon. The basket seemed to float in front of him just like the turkey.

"Stop it right now!" demanded Trine as he watched the gypsy drop the basket next to the turkey. The gypsy returned to the wagon again and grabbed a big ham. "I have this ax and I'm not afraid to use it!" shouted Trine as he held up the ax with both hands. Actually, he was afraid to use it. He had never harmed anyone in his life.

Berk tossed the ham into the pile by the side of the road. "You can't see me! You can't see me!" Berk taunted, dancing back and forth like a little child. Trine could clearly see and smell this huge, hairy man. He thought this gypsy must be insane.

Berk walked back to the wagon again. As he came closer, Trine swung the ax at the gypsy, but he ducked just in time and the ax only grazed his shoulder. Trine found himself falling forward because he missed his target. He did not want to severely hurt the gypsy. He only wanted to stop him from stealing his food. As Trine fell forward, the gypsy punched him hard and square in the face with his huge fist. The grocer fell backwards and was knocked unconscious.

Berk laughed again and said, "See, you can't see me!" He lifted a large box from the wagon and walked back to the pile of food on the side of the road. He dropped the box there with everything else he had taken.

"How will I get all this stuff back to camp?" he said, scratching his head. "I know!" He pulled the key out of his pocket, shut his eyes and said, "I wish I had a wagon! I wish I had a wagon!" When he opened his eyes there it was, a large grocer's wagon. "It worked again!" he cried. He grabbed the ham under one arm and the basket in the other. He placed them back in the wagon. He lifted the box and put it in the wagon as well. Then he went back for the turkey. He tossed it into the compartment and slammed the doors shut.

He stopped for a moment to look at the unconscious man lying in the road. "Never saw me comin', did ya? Ha, ha!" He laughed.

Berk strained his huge muscles and lifted one end of the branch that blocked the road. He lugged it over to the side of the road and dropped it. Then he heaved up the other end of the branch and moved it off the road as well. He got into the front seat of the wagon, and with a whip, he coaxed the horses to head toward the gypsy camp.

"It's magic, it is," he said out loud, "and it works every time!" He was so excited he did not even notice the green chain that was now around his neck or the lizard that jumped up onto the seat next to him.

CHAPTER 15

The Evening Meal

Ben brought Litfim back to the orphanage just in time for supper that evening. As soon as Lady Elaine saw him, she hugged the boy and told him to go into the dining hall to get something to eat. "You will report to my office immediately after supper," she said to him sternly. He hung his head as he walked into the dining hall. He knew he was in trouble, but he was glad to be home.

"He has quite a story to tell this time, My Lady," Ben said to Lady Elaine.

"He always has quite a story to tell, Captain." Lady Elaine always used people's titles because they always addressed her by her title. She thought it was only proper to return the honor.

"This time, he might have come across something very important. Would you mind if I allowed Loremaster Ebesian to ask him some questions?"

"Loremaster Ebesian! Why would he want to talk to Litfim?" the Lady asked, wondering what the boy had gotten himself into now.

"I believe Litfim might know something that will help the loremaster in his current quest. If I am right, it could be extremely significant."

"Did Litfim steal something from the loremaster or his students?" Lady Elaine asked anxiously.

"No, he is not in trouble, My Lady. But in his wanderings, he may have discovered an important piece of information that the loremaster needs to know."

"If that is the case, then by all means, tell Ebesian he is welcome to speak to the boy. But remember, Litfim has a habit of telling very tall tales, Captain."

*   *   *   *   *

Sasha walked from wagon to wagon and tent to tent in the gypsy camp distributing hot bowls of soup. She felt it was her responsibility to make sure that her neighbors, especially the oldest and the youngest ones, had enough to eat. Almost every week, Magnus, the owner of the *White Stallion*, would make more soup than he knew he could sell. At closing time, he would say to Sasha, "Please take this soup off my hands. I can't store it. It will just go bad. If you take it home with you, it will be a great help to me." He knew that Sasha lived among those who were poor. He also knew that she was hard working and generous. So he gave her food from time to time, knowing it would help to feed her small community among the gypsy wagons.

Sasha set two bowls of soup down in front of an elderly lady and her sister. "You're a treasure, Sasha," the old lady lisped through a toothless grin.

Sasha smiled and said, "Oh, it's nothing, Hala. Enjoy it!" Sasha lifted a tattered blanket over the old lady's shoulder and gently patted her on the back. Hala smiled back at her, her heart warmed by the simple act of affection.

As she went back to the kettle of soup on the fire at the center of the camp, Stang walked over, but he did not say anything. He took off his black leather gloves and warmed his hands over the fire. Sasha cautiously looked up at him. He frightened her. He frightened everyone. Maybe that was why he was their leader. No one would dare challenge his authority, because he had a reputation for being ruthless.

Sasha filled another bowl and held it toward him. "Would you like some soup, sir?" she asked quietly, almost holding her breath.

He looked down at her for a moment. He saw the fear in her bright eyes. He saw how the hand holding the bowl trembled. Even though he was hungry, he looked away from her and said in a low voice, "No, thank you. Make sure everyone in the camp has what they need."

As Stang turned and walked away from her, he hated himself. He felt regret over what he had become—a feared assassin. Even the people he loved and swore to protect were terrified in his presence. He cared about Sasha like a daughter, and he would never harm her. He deeply appreciated her kindness to his people. She always shared food and clothing with everyone in the camp. Without her, they would not have survived. He wished that she could see that he cared for them just as deeply as she did. Instead, she thought he was a monster.

He reminded himself that he had to be a monster. Who else would protect his people from the constant threats around them? Stang thought back to a year ago when he was making his evening rounds through the camp. He heard two men in a tent talking about Sasha's good looks. The one man was boasting to the other that he was going to ravish her that night, because he knew she would be alone. Stang waited in the shadows outside of the tent for over an hour. When the man came out of the tent, Stang stealthily followed him. As the man reached the steps to Sasha's wagon, Stang quickly grabbed him from behind. With one hand, he covered the man's mouth, and with the other hand, he plunged a large knife deep into the man's back. He dragged the man's body off into the woods, and he was never seen again. *I am a ruthless killer*, Stang thought, *but it's for the good of those under my care. Even if they've misunderstood my motives, what I've done is just and right.* With those thoughts, he consoled himself and he continued his walk around the camp.

CHAPTER 16

The Important Question

Litfim sat alone, pouting in a chair in Lady Elaine's office. She just told him that he had lost all of his privileges for a month and he was not to leave the orphanage under any circumstances. Then she told him to wait there until she came back, and that he was to spend the time thinking about what he had done wrong. *I almost got killed—twice*, he thought. *Wasn't that punishment enough?*

Fifteen minutes later, Lady Elaine came back into the office followed by Captain Ben and an old man with a long gray beard. She said, "This is Loremaster Ebesian, Litfim. He is a very important man. He wants to ask you some questions about what happened to you. You are not in trouble. He just wants you to help him by giving him some information. Do you understand?"

Litfim nodded his head.

The old man sat down across from him, smiled at him and said, "So I heard you had quite an adventure over the last two days. Can you tell me about it?"

The old man was not as frightening as the lunatic or Stang, but he was somehow more intimidating. Here sat a powerful, wise man with immense authority asking him questions about what he had done. Litfim felt overwhelmed by guilt. He looked down at the floor and started crying.

"Ah, my son! It's all right," Ebesian said, putting his hand on the boy's shoulder. "You're safe now, and all is forgiven. I just want to make sure that King Tavon's side wins. You want that as well, right?"

65

"You serve King Tavon?" Litfim said, as he stopped sobbing.

"Of course! Loremasters are Tavon's servants. We teach every-one to follow his ways. You have absolutely nothing to fear from me."

"But I know what I did was wrong. I almost got killed—twice!"

"Yes, I know what that's like. I 'almost got killed' seventy-seven times," the old man said with a very serious expression.

"What did you do to not get killed?"

"I prayed to the Highest One, and he rescued me."

"So did I," Litfim said, his voice expressing excitement now.

"And that's why you're safe and sound right now."

Litfim wiped his face with his sleeve, and said, "What do you want to know?"

"Tell us about your adventure."

Litfim tried to remember what he said to Stang. Telling the truth worked with the scary gypsy, so being completely honest with the powerful loremaster would probably work as well.

"I went to this really big, wrecked house. I thought no one was there, but a crazy man chased me. I ran away, but there was a wall, so I ran into the house. I saw a key on a desk. It changed colors and disappeared. The man chased me and I ran away. I walked down the road and saw some gypsies. They gave me something to drink and I fell asleep. When I woke up, they had the key. They said the key was in my pocket, but I don't know how it got there. They made me take them back to the wrecked house. They looked around and then they left me there." *There, the whole story, the whole truth,* he thought.

But then he added, "Oh wait, then Anskar woke me up and told me two men were looking for me. Captain Ben and another man brought me home. The end." *There, the real whole story, the real whole truth,* he thought.

Ben asked, "Who is Anskar?"

"A friend. He helps me out from time to time."

"What does he look like?" Ben asked eagerly.

"He's tall, kinda big and strong . . ."

"Tell us more about the *key*," Ebesian interrupted, looking sternly at Ben.

It was clear that Ebesian thought that Ben was failing to see what was really important in this conversation. He was diverting the boy's thoughts off on an unnecessary tangent. Besides, what did this windship captain know about the Lore in comparison to him? Ben thought his questions about the mysterious Anskar were essential in several ways, but it was clear that it was not the time nor the place to challenge the loremaster.

Litfim said, "It was all bent and green, and then it became straight and purple."

"Was it bent and green when the gypsies held it?" Ebesian asked.

"Yes."

"But when you touched the key it became straight and violet?"

"Ye—yes," Litfim said hesitantly. He did not know if touching it was something he was permitted do.

"Ah, my boy! This is good news! Where is it now?" Ebesian said, smiling broadly.

"The gypsies have it, I guess."

"Do you know were these gypsies are?"

"Yes, they're in the wood off the South Road."

"And where is this big house where you found the key?"

"It's just a little further down the road. Right on the cliff across the fjord from the City."

"You mean the City of Babbelar?"

"Yeah."

"You did well, my son! I'll see if Lady Elaine might be able to give you back a few of your lost privileges."

Litfim smiled a big smile. *This honesty thing really works. I'm never, ever going to lie again,* he thought.

A small gecko was stuck to the ceiling just above their heads. It heard the entire conversation that took place in Lady Elaine's office. When everyone left the room, the gecko scurried out into the darkness. It had much to report to its master, the Dragon.

CHAPTER 17

The Narrowed Search

After speaking to Litfim, Ebesian gathered Ben, Nathan, Mandar, and his students together in a small room at the orphanage. He wanted to tell them all that the violet key, the Murastan, had been found. On a table, he spread out an ancient map.

"A young boy from this orphanage came into contact with the Murastan yesterday," Ebesian said to the group. "But it has fallen into the hands of a group of gypsies who live just south of here in the woods."

Landron said, "How will we get it from the gypsies? They will not just allow us to search through their belongings, especially if they know that the key is powerful."

"We must find someone who has access to the gypsy's camp," Ebesian responded.

"We may know of someone," Ben said sheepishly, glancing at his brother.

"Good! We will have to meet with that person as soon as possible," Ebesian said. "What is his name?"

"Her name is Sasha," Nathan answered. "She is a Tavonian who lives at the gypsy camp."

"Excellent!" Ebesian continued. "We need to speak to her as soon as possible." He pushed the map into the middle of the table. "The boy said that he initially found the key in a broken-down mansion. From my research, I believe he has stumbled upon the location of the Beacon of the Murastan, which is right here." He pointed to a place on the map. "It is right across the fjord from the City of Babbelar, which is exactly where the boy first saw the key. Of course, the ancient tower is now hidden under ruins and later construction, but it is still there. We just have to find the entrance to it."

"Did the boy touch the key?" asked Traven.

"Yes," Ebesian answered, "but just for a moment with his hand and not with a sword."

"Why is that important—that he touched it?" Nathan asked.

"Each of the seven keys will meld with any Tavonian blade," Traven explained. "Once a key binds to a sword, it is there until that person dies. That person becomes the guardian of that key and can use it to do great things for the Kingdom of Tavon."

"And you don't think that Litfim would be a worthy guardian of something so important," countered Nathan.

Traven shook his head and said, "No, you don't understand. It's not up to us to decide who should receive a key. The Highest One chooses who will bear each of the keys. We just want to know who has the keys so that we can be sure that they will use them to unlock and rekindle the seven beacons."

Nathan counted the students in the room and said, "And you hope that the seven of you will become the guardians of the keys! Isn't that why Ebesian brought you all here?"

"If that is the will of the Highest One," Traven said with confidence. "Otherwise, we need to persuade all the guardians to work together so that the lights will be restored."

"But first we have to find them all," Tasca said.

"That sounds impossible!" Nathan said, throwing his hands up in the air.

"'Nothing is impossible for the Highest One!'"[1] Ebesian quoted from the Lore. "We *will* find all seven of the keys, and most, if not all of the guardians will be those of you who are standing here right now. Of that I am certain!"

Nathan still thought the task was an impossible one, but Ben wondered how he himself might be tied to the destiny of the keys.

---

[1] Matthew 19:26.

CHAPTER 18

The Dragon's Throne

Although it is now hard to imagine, the nekron were once like the engven. Originally, they were pure in heart and tall and handsome, but when they rebelled against the Highest One, they became wicked to the core and reptilian in appearance. A great battle took place, and the nekron were driven out of Ehadreon and cast down to Varden. Although the nekron could not touch or use the seven keys because they were forged in Ehadreon, they persuaded Varden's first inhabitants to twist and misuse them in ways Tavon never intended. The nekron then became even more twisted and cursed as well. Thousands of years of bondage to evil had a profound effect on their saurian bodies and their wicked minds. Everything about them had been totally corrupted. They knew that they were doomed to suffer everlasting misery in the Abyss for their evil and rebellion, so out of spite, they now sought to share that terrible fate with as many Vardenians as possible.

Hundreds of miles to the east of Sugstal was what used to be the Kingdom of Lisendore. It was once a vibrant land of wooded mountains, crisscrossed by clear streams and waterfalls, inhabited by hundreds of ibexes and thousands of kinds of colorful birds. It had some of the richest farm land in all of Varden, with the farms perched on wide terraces across the mountainsides around beautiful fjords. That was before the Beacon of Lisendore was extinguished by the Enemy. Now it was a place stripped bare of all life and vegetation. Dark, rocky crags and polluted waters were all that was left of Lisendore.

That was why it was now called The Darklands by those in the west, and Norgar by those in the league with the Enemy. All its people had fled to other lands, fugitives of the Great War. Its Grand Palace was now a mere ruin, its renown and splendor gone forever. The last heir to its throne, Andelsar, was rumored to be dead. The other members of his royal house were scattered across Varden. Now only the nekron haunted the barren rocks of Lisendore. Seated on the throne of this once great kingdom was the one known as the Great Dragon, who was the leader of the nekron. He sat alone in the darkness until his servants come to report to him.

A two-foot-long lizard sat trembling in the darkness of the great hall of Lisendore, waiting to be called in to the throne room to speak with the Dragon. It had a black chain around its neck that was also attached to two stunted legs on its right side. His name was Lacertus, but he had gained the nickname of Muraworm because he spent most of his time guarding the yellow-green key—the Murastan.

A small gecko emerged from the throne room. As it scurried past Lacertus, it squeaked, "You are in big trouble with the boss! Ha-ha!"

Lacertus was trembling with both anger and fear. He felt anger toward the gecko, because it reported all that it had heard back at the orphanage in Sugstal to the Dragon. He felt fear at the thought of having to face the Dragon and answer for what had happened.

As the gecko moved toward the doorway out of the great hall, Lacertus pounced on it and quickly grabbed it with his mouth. The gecko screamed in pain and pleaded, "Let me go! The Great One will be angry if you don't!" But Lacertus was not feeling merciful to this traitor. He bit down hard on the gecko with a loud crunch. After a few more crunches, Lacertus swallowed it down, and the gecko was no more. *If only the Dragon was so easy to handle,* he thought as he entered the throne room.

He ran in quickly. The Dragon must not be kept waiting. Lacertus cautiously approached the throne, realizing the Dragon could do to him far worse than what he had just done to the gecko. Standing up on his hind legs, he bowed down low and then he fell onto all four of his feet.

The Dragon was ten feet tall with thick, black scales. It had feet and a tail like an alligator, and wings like a bat that spread out twelve feet wide. It sat on the throne with a bent and tarnished crown on its horned head. Smoke emerged from its nostrils, and a dark mist surrounded the throne.

"Muraworm, I'm not happy!" the Dragon growled.

"Yes, but the key is still safe, Great One," Lacertus said with as much confidence as he could muster.

"I've been told that the enemy is close to finding it. It must not fall into their hands."

"No, of course not. What do you suggest we do, Great One?" Lacertus was visibly shaking now, and hoping he was saying the right words to appease the Dragon.

"The key must be moved to a place where it will be harder to find. A place where greed is so common the Murastan would be difficult to spot."

"A place like Corasar?" Lacertus asked.

"Yes, Corasar is perfect! Find an extremely greedy Corasarian to move the key to safety. Use the fool who speaks of the Enemy wanting them to be wealthy to get it there. Do you understand my orders?"

"Yes, Great One," Lacertus croaked.

"Good! Get the key back to Corasar. Do not fail me, or there will be serious consequences. Now go! Get away from me before I decide to devour you the way you ate the gecko!" the Dragon commanded.

Lacertus bowed again and backed out of the throne room, bowing yet again when he got to the doorway. He ran through the great hall and out of the palace as quickly as his little legs would carry him. He did not want to wait for the Dragon to change his mind.

When the throne room was empty again, the Dragon let down his facade. He was weary from trying to sustain his masquerade, so he transformed back into what he truly looked like. As the mist and the smoke disappeared, so did the size, the scales, the wings and the horns. Instead, the "Great One" appeared to be a lizard not much larger than Lacertus. At some time in the past, its head had been crushed, but it had survived what appeared to be a mortal wound.

A heavy, black chain wound around its throat and entire body. The chain was so large the lizard could no longer move off the throne because of the immense weight it had to carry. It let out a blood-curdling scream because of the pain it endured, and the sound of it echoed through the darkness.

Lacertus stopped for a moment on his flight out of the ruins of the palace when he heard the scream. *Another poor victim of the Dragon was being tortured,* he thought. Little did he realize that the victim was the Dragon himself!

CHAPTER 19

The Day of Resting

It was the Day of Resting. Sasha took her best white dress out of her closet and carefully laid it on the bed. She gently ran her hand over the colorful embroidery. It had been lovingly sewn a few years ago by her mother as a gift for her seventeenth birthday. Tears welled up in her eyes as she thought of her mother's smile and laughter. "I miss you, mama!" she whispered.

Sasha quickly ate some jam and bread. She washed her face and hands in the basin on top of the dresser. Looking in the mirror, she carefully braided her long, dark hair, and then she put on the favorite dress and her best boots. She went back to the dresser and took a bright, violet sword out of the top drawer. After putting on her white wool jacket, she placed the sword in a scabbard that she slid over her left shoulder. Then she stepped out of her wagon into the brisk, morning air.

As she began walking through the camp, she said hello to a small group of women who were cooking breakfast over a fire. They warmly greeted her, and she gave them a winsome smile. When she reached the edge of the camp, she saw Stang leaning against a tree. She put her head down and quickened her pace slightly as she walked past him.

"Going to pray again, Sasha?" Stang asked in his gravelly voice. "You're wearing your white dress."

"Yes, I am," she said confidently as she passed by where he was standing.

"Will you pray for me, lass?" he said in a very quiet, honest-sounding tone.

She stopped walking and turned back to look at him. "Are you serious? Or are you mocking me?"

He looked at her for a moment with his stern eyes. They had become bluer in color. Rather than their usual red, they appeared to be purple. Then he looked down, and he turned away and walked back toward the camp without saying another word.

As Sasha watched him walk away, she shouted, "Yes, yes I will!"

Stang stood still for a moment, but he did not turn back to look at her.

"Yes, I will," Sasha said again more quietly.

A single tear ran down Stang's face, but Sasha never saw it. He just kept walking back to the camp without looking back at her. She watched him walk away for a moment, and then she headed toward the prayerhouse in the northern part of Sugstal.

CHAPTER 20

The Day of Games

The Corasarians were a short, rotund race of people, who really knew how to enjoy themselves. They loved to cook, bake and eat, and they produced an abundance of sweet foods. All they ever talked about were parties, plays and entertainments. Of course, all of these events involved drinking large amounts of wine and beer, and eating massive quantities of fine meats and delicious pastries, cakes, and desserts. They never really stopped eating except to sleep, which was also one of their favorite pastimes.

They spent a lot of time talking about shopping, the finest clothing, and how they furnished their large, comfortable houses. Actually, by law, all of the houses in the capital city of Babbelar had to look alike. The only minor difference between them was how they are painted. Most of them were a variation of beige or yellow green. Ebesian once said, "The Corasarians' love of conformity and comfort causes me to be sick. But I don't think they would notice because it's the same color as all of their buildings."

The prime minister of Corasar once possessed the yellow-green key—the Murastan. After using it for many years, he believed that he could still tap into its power, even if it was not in his possession. So he sold it to the highest bidder at an auction at the Corasarian Parliament. The Murastan was circulated among so many people in Corasar that it thoroughly affected everything in their culture and society. Over time, the Murastan was removed from Corasar, yet the entire nation still continued to experience its devastating effects.

When outsiders were asked to describe the Corasarians they often said, "They all look alike," and "They are all far too fat." The Corasarians found this characterization offensive. They believed the worst thing a person could do was to be negative and diminish someone else's sense of worth. They preferred to think of themselves as "pleasantly plump." Their round shape was really something to be envied, because it was a sign of their happiness and prosperity. They believed that others made fun of their appearance out of jealousy. "Corasarians are built for comfort and pleasure," they said, and it was true. Yet the Lore taught discipline and self-sacrifice. Perhaps that was why so few people in Corasar believed in the Lore, or even understood it.

It was the Day of Resting in Corasar as well, but most of them worked every day of the week and never rested, so they called it the Day of Games instead. On this day of the week, the chubby little children of Corasar played games outside in a vain attempt to show they were physically fit, and the adults watched athletic contests in stadiums as they ate large helpings of sweet and salty foods, all washed down with large amounts of beer.

On this Day of Games, thousands of Corasarians were gathered together in a semicircular amphitheater to hear their favorite teacher speak. His name was Telecon. Telecon had curly, white hair as thick as lamb's wool, and a long nose that gave him a wolf-like appearance. Some considered Telecon to be follower of King Tavon, but he clearly taught things that conflicted with the Lore. Telecon told the wealthy Corasarians exactly what they wanted to hear, and it made him very wealthy as well. He held their values and understood what they considered to be the most important aspects of life. The heavy green chain he wore around his neck, bound to each of his wrists, was a clear indication he was one of them. His beady yellow-green eyes showed that he had embraced their values for many years.

"The Great One wants you to have many houses and fields— gold and silver!" Telecon said, as he walked back and forth across the stage. "The only reason you don't have them is because you don't believe they are already yours! You've allowed negative words and negative thinking to poison your mind," he said, pointing to his own wolf-like head with both hands.

The thousands who were packed into the amphitheater nodded their heads in agreement with everything Telecon said. They hung on his every word and smiled broadly at his teaching that greed was the highest of all virtues. What they did not see was the small chameleon that clung to the back of Telecon's neck. It had changed its colors to blend in perfectly with Telecon's green clothing and white hair. Every word Telecon spoke were the words the chameleon whispered in his ear. They also did not see Lacertus, nervously pacing back and forth backstage on his little, lizard legs. He had told the chameleon on Telecon's neck what the Dragon had ordered them to do. Now he was desperately hoping their plan would work.

"Say it! Say it!" Lacertus hissed as he nervously bit his claws offstage. "Tell the idiots already!"

"You show you believe by taking action," the chameleon whispered to Telecon.

"You show you believe by taking action!" Telecon shouted to the crowd.

"Let's say the Great One has a forest he wants you to own," whispered the chameleon.

"Let's say the Great One has a forest he wants you to own," repeated Telecon to his listeners.

"If you really believe he wants you to have it, you have to actually go and claim it!" the chameleon said in his ear.

"If you really believe he wants you to have it, you have to actually go and claim it!" parroted Telecon.

"Good, now tell them where to go!" Lacertus impatiently hissed from the side of the stage.

"Let's say that forest was in Spysar! That means you actually have to get on a windship and go there!" the chameleon said, with Telecon repeating every word to the thousands listening. "How else would you show you believe the forest is yours? That's what the Lore means when it says, 'Belief without action is dead!'"[2]

---

[2] James 2:17 and 26.

Sitting in the crowd were Arboron and Histrionicah. Arboron loved to hear Telecon speak, and he often told his friends and business associates that he had become very wealthy by following Telecon's teachings. The weighty, green chain around Arboron's neck grew heavier, and the warts across his flabby face grew larger. He looked even more like the large toad that now sat under his seat in the amphitheater. As Telecon spoke, the toad croaked to Arboron, "He's talking about you, my friend!"

Arboron thought what he heard the toad say was actually in his own head. He always thought that the toad's statements where ideas he himself had generated in his own mind. He boasted to others how these great insights had made him a billionaire.

"He's talking about me!" Arboron gleefully whispered in his wife's ear. "As soon as we leave here, I'm going to book passage to Sugstal in Spysar!"

The rotund, green-haired woman sitting next to him smiled and looked down at the diamonds and jewels glittering on all ten of her pale, chubby fingers. Histrionicah admired them for a moment and said, "Sounds good to me, honey! I believe!"

CHAPTER 21

The Prayerhouse

The bell in the tower was ringing loudly, calling those in Sugstal to come and pray. People greeted Sasha with warm hugs as she entered the prayerhouse. The large, wooden building sat about half way between the orphanage and Ansen's windship yard. Today, the place was packed with people because everyone heard that Ebesian was going to speak. The balcony was usually empty most weeks, but today it was already full. Ebesian's students sat on the right side of the U-shaped balcony. Ansen, Ben and Nathan sat on the left side of the balcony, across from the students. Lady Elaine and many of the orphans sat in the back of the balcony. Ebesian stood in the front of the room by the platform, greeting everyone who wanted to talk to him. Sasha quickly sat down in her usual seat on the main floor, two rows from the platform. She did not want to have to stand in the back because of the unusually large crowd. The three hundred people who were gathered there were all talking loudly and laughing as they conversed with one another. The place was filled with joy, not solemnity. No one noticed the tall woodsman who entered the building after everyone was inside, except for young Litfim, who made room for the engven warrior to sit on the bench next to him.

"Welcome, friends!" said Mandar after he walked onto the platform. He raised his hands, and as everyone quieted down, they also sat down if they could find a seat. "Today we will have the honor to hear our good friend, Loremaster Ebesian, share his wisdom and insights from the Lore with us. But first we will pray and ask the Highest One to show us his will for our lives."

Soon the room was filled again with sound as people gathered together in groups of three or four to pray. Sasha remembered her promise, and she prayed for Stang. She prayed for all of the people in the gypsy camp by name, recalling specific needs they each had, earnestly asking that they would understand the Truth. She lastly prayed for herself, asking to know what purpose she would serve in the High King's plan. When she finished praying, peace flooded over her heart, and she knew her prayers were already being answered.

From the back of the room, someone started singing with a deep baritone voice. Soon others joined in, and the entire congregation began singing praises to the Highest One. For hours, they sang with exuberance. During the singing, many threw their Tavonian swords in the air in celebration. They glowed violet, blue, azure, cyan, jade, emerald and bright white. Although in other worlds edged weapons might be dangerous to throw over one's head, they knew that swords forged in Ehadreon can never harm those loyal to the Highest King of that Land.

Then Loremaster Ebesian stepped up onto the platform to speak. He stood there for a moment looking over the congregation, and he prayed for the words to say to the people. He straightened out his robes and put his hand in his pocket. He took out the puzzle box he always carried with him, and he carefully placed it on the lectern. Next to it he laid his sword which glowed with a soft white light. Then he began to read from the worn Lorebook in front of him:

"'Godliness is a means of great gain when it goes hand in hand with contentment. Since we brought nothing into this world, we can take nothing out of it. So if we have food and shelter, we should be satisfied with that. But those who desire to have a substantial fortune fall into temptation and a snare, and into many foolish and harmful lusts which cause them to sink into ruin and destruction. For the love of money is a root of all evils, and by craving it some people have wandered far from the Lore and brought upon themselves many heartaches.'"[3]

---

[3] 1 Timothy 6:6–10.

Ebesian looked up from the book and said, "Many people today sadly believe the lie that wealth can buy happiness. They run after money thinking that it will somehow bring them the pleasure they are longing for down deep inside. Yet they have set their hearts on things that are empty, temporary and fleeting. So their lives become empty and meaningless as they become enslaved to their own hollow desires and evil lusts. They fill their lives with pain and misery as they fill them up with worthless things. Eventually, they discover that their pursuit of riches has left them completely bankrupt of the things that are truly important—the things that give a person eternal worth. They give away their very souls for a worthless pile of rust and ash!

"My brothers and sisters, the secret to knowing real satisfaction in this world is simple. If you have enough food, clothes on your back, and a roof over your head, be content with that. Then find true, lasting pleasure and worth by giving everything else you have away! That is what our King Tavon did. He is the rightful heir to the throne of all of Varden. But when the keys that governed this world were bent and misused, the Enemy usurped his throne. Tavon gave up all of the wealth of his kingdom, and even his very life, to rescue us from our own evil desires and the Enemy's power. Now he calls for us to do the same. He is building a new kingdom, built on compassion and generosity. If you give freely so that the needs of others might be met, he will reward you for it when he returns in power and restores his kingdom! And, most importantly, instead of being enslaved and destroyed by your own evil desires, you will know the freedom and joy that comes from loving the way our King loves us!"

Sasha smiled contentedly as she listened to Ebesian speak. His words were a great encouragement to her. A few evenings ago, she had been thinking about how little she owned or would ever own, and she began to feel sorry for herself. *It's not such a bad thing to be a poor gypsy girl,* she thought. *Not bad at all!*

* * * * *

As Sasha left the prayerhouse, Ben happened to walk out at the same time. "Hello, Bensareon," she said smiling at him.

"Hi, Sasha," Ben responded. He noticed she looked very beautiful in her white dress.

"Oh, so you *do* know my name!" she teased.

"Of course, I do. Why would you think I didn't?"

"Because every time I talk to you, you act like I'm invisible."

"I'm sorry! I guess I get too caught up in my work."

"Or you're in love with someone else!" Sasha said, smiling confidently.

Ben suddenly felt very uncomfortable, so he said, "By the way, Loremaster Ebesian discovered that orphan boy, Litfim, came into contact with one of the seven keys the other day."

"Why are you changing the subject?" she asked, smiling and taking hold of his arm.

Ben noticed that a wonderful scent surrounded her, like the fragrance of the violet Ehadre-el flowers he remembered from when he was a boy. He blushed when she came close to him, and he said, "Because it's important that you know that Litfim said that a gypsy now has the key."

"And gypsies are known to be thieves, and since I'm a gypsy, maybe I stole it!" she said sarcastically and still smiling.

"No! Ebus, I mean Loremaster Ebesian, was looking for someone who might be able to keep an eye out for the key at, uh, your camp." He made sure he did not use the word *gypsy* again.

"So he can find out what *other* gypsy stole it!" she kidded with a big smile.

"Sasha, this is serious! A lot is at stake here!"

"I know. I'm just having a little fun with you, Ben." She kissed him firmly on the cheek, and Ben turned bright red. Walking away backwards from him, she said, "Maybe I'll be the one who finds this key before anyone else!" Then she smiled brightly and turned to walk briskly home.

Ben smiled and thought, *She's wonderful. Why didn't I notice that before?*

CHAPTER 22

The Fortune Teller

As Sasha walked through the gypsy camp, a middle-aged woman with yellow-green eyes waved her over to her tent.

"Yoo-hoo! Sasha! Yoo-hoo!" Calypso shouted. "Come here for a minute. I need to talk to you."

Sasha hesitatingly walked over to Calypso's tent. Sasha usually avoided the fortune teller, because she was known to be a vicious gossiper, and people claimed she practiced witchcraft.

"Come in! Don't be afraid!" Calypso cooed, as she waved for Sasha to enter.

As Sasha cautiously stepped inside the tent, she immediately felt an evil presence. Creepy paintings of snakes and weird amulets hung everywhere. Bizarre statues of creatures with multiple arms and legs sat on pedestals all around the tent. The strong smell of incense could not cover the putrid smell of something dead. Even though it was the early afternoon, and dozens of candles were lit, the darkness inside the tent seemed to be devouring all the light around it. The sword on Sasha's back began to blaze with a bright, violet light.

Calypso's daughter Hexah sat at a round, wooden table covered with a cloth with strange symbols painted on it. She shuffled a stack of sinister looking cards. A large, black chain hung from both of her wrists. Hexah was a hunchback. Ever since she was a little girl, she had a large hump on her back. Since her eyes were completely coal black, most people thought Hexah was totally blind.

"We wanted to thank you for all your generosity," Calypso said in a sugary sweet tone. "You've been so nice, giving people food all the time. We wanted to thank you by reading your fortune."

"Oh, no thanks!" Sasha said, shaking her head and backing away. "I don't believe in fortune telling. You know I serve Tavon."

"But we insist!" Hexah whined in her shrill voice.

When Sasha tried to turn to walk out of the tent, Calypso blocked her path. Hexah started turning over the strange cards and placing them in rows on the table. One showed a frightened couple getting married and the other showed a gaunt mother surrounded by hungry children.

"You will marry a handsome windship captain," she whined. "And you will have many children and a long life."

"I have to go!" Sasha insisted, trying again to get past Calypso.

Hexah turned over two more cards. One showed the picture of a twisted key and the other a cloaked skeleton wielding a large scythe. "Unless you pursue the key of power. Then you will surely die!"

"I'm leaving right now!" Sasha said firmly as she pushed her way past Calypso.

"Have a nice day, Sasha!" Calypso said with a sinister smile as Sasha ran out the door of the tent.

* * * * *

About an hour later, Jon and Traven walked into the gypsy camp with their swords hidden under their capes. Loremaster Ebesian had sent them there to see if they could discover the whereabouts of the key. He thought that of all of his students, they would attract the least attention among the gypsies. As they walked through the camp, Calypso noticed them and waved them over to her tent.

"You handsome, young men looking for something?" Calypso cooed. "Perhaps I can help you! Come in! Come in!"

Traven looked at Jon and whispered, "What do you think she wants from us?"

"I don't know," Jon whispered back. "Let's go over and find out."

As Jon walked toward Calypso's tent, Traven said, "Are you sure about this?" Then he shook his head and followed Jon inside the mysterious tent.

When Traven stepped inside, he immediately felt an evil presence there. Under his breath he said, "I knew this was a bad idea!"

"This is my daughter, Hexah," Calypso said as she pointed toward the table. "She has the gift and is able to answer any question you might have, about the past or the future."

"Well, then she can tell me what my question is!" Jon stated skeptically. He also felt there was an evil presence in the tent.

"Yes, I can!" Hexah whined in a creepy voice. She shuffled her strange cards and started placing them in rows on the table. Traven noticed the large hump on Hexah's back. He also saw a forked tongue flick out of the hump toward Hexah's ear.

"You will marry a princess from the house of Saren," Hexah moaned as she looked up at Jon with her pitch-black eyes.

"Really? What is her name?" Jon asked.

"Her name is Tasca, daughter of Benton."

"How do you know that?" Jon asked a bit surprised.

"My spirit guide tells me all things," Hexah whined. "You look for a special key, but it is not here. It has been taken far away. Yes, it has now passed into the Darklands!"

Jon looked at Traven. He did not know what to say. Traven just looked back at Hexah's hump. He could plainly see the nekron there now, clinging to her back. She was simply parroting everything it told her to say. Actually, it was using her body as if it were its own.

Calypso held out her hand toward Jon and said, "That will be five of your kroners, please."

"We don't have any money," Traven said. "But what treasure we do have we are willing to share with you."

Traven stepped closer to the table and unsheathed his sword. Calypso's face suddenly went pale, as a look of terror filled her yellow-green eyes.

"In the name of King Tavon, I set you free!" Traven shouted as he swung his sword across the table. The sword passed harmlessly through Hexah's body, but the nekron on her back exploded into a cloud of thick, black smoke. The girl fell out of her chair and Traven bent down to help her up.

"What have you done?" screamed Calypso. "You wicked men have destroyed my livelihood and my daughter's life!" Calypso started pounding her fists on Jon's chest, and he grabbed her wrists to restrain her.

Hexah's eyes were no longer black but sky blue. The hump on her back was gone. Traven said to her, "If you truly desire to be free from your chains, turn your back on all evil, and swear allegiance to King Tavon. He loves you and he will deliver you. Do you believe that?"

"Yes, I do," Hexah said in a clear voice. It was her own voice now, different from the one she had spoken with before. "Please, King Tavon, set me free!"

The dark chain between her wrists fell to the ground and disappeared. In its place, she now wore two silver bands, and a short sword appeared at her feet. Tears flowed down her cheeks from eyes that were now violet. Traven helped her to her feet. She hugged him and said, "Thank you!"

"Don't thank me. Thank King Tavon. He has set you free!" Traven said with tears filling his eyes.

Calypso stopped hitting Jon and screamed at her daughter, "What have you done? No! You can't be one of *them*!" She tried to slap her daughter, but Jon stopped her by grabbing her hand. "I'm going to tell everyone in the camp what you did," she shouted at Traven. "When they get their hands on the two of you, they'll lynch you!" Then she ran out of the tent and started shouting, "Help! Help! These men have attacked my daughter and stolen her gift by evil magic! Help! Help!"

Jon turned to Hexah and said, "There is a young woman named Sasha here. Do you know her?"

"Yes, she lives in a wagon just a few yards from here," Hexah answered.

"We need to see her! Now!" Jon said. "I don't think your mother is very happy with us right now! Is there another way out of this tent?"

"Follow me!" Hexah said.

Jon and Traven followed Hexah out of the back door of the tent, and they ran toward Sasha's wagon. A group of people started gathering on the other side of the tent. They were listening to Calypso tell a story about how two men from the village had cast an evil spell over her daughter and chased her spirit guide away. She claimed the men then beat her and stole all her money, and they were still in the camp.

Jon knocked on the door of Sasha's wagon. When she opened the door, Jon said, "In the name of King Tavon we need your help!"

"Come in!" Sasha said looking worried.

When they were all inside, Sasha closed the door and said, "What's the matter?"

Jon said, "We are two of Loremaster Ebesian's students. We just helped this girl gain her freedom from a nekron that was on her back."

Sasha looked intently at the girl and asked, "Is that you, Hexah?"

"Yes," the girl said, "but my real name is Melantha. They called me Hexah after the lizard took control of me."

Sasha looked into her eyes. She saw the girl's eyes were now violet instead of pitch-black. She also took Melantha's hands in hers. She saw the silver bands where the black manacles used to be. "And now you're free!" Sasha said with tears in her eyes.

"Yes, King Tavon delivered me!" Melantha said. Sasha hugged her tightly.

Outside the wagon, men were shouting. Jon pushed the curtain aside and looked out the window. People were running around and searching with angry expressions on their faces and clubs in their hands.

Jon dropped the curtain and said, "It looks like we have upset Melantha's mother. A crowd is forming outside, and I don't think they're happy we put an end to her fortune telling business."

"The key must be very close by or the enemy would not be giving us such a hard time," Traven said to everyone. Then he asked Melantha, "Do you know where it is?"

"No, but I know that it is close by. I think one of Stang's men has it." Melantha tried to remember his name. "It is hard for me to remember what the lizard said to me. It took over control of my mind and I tried to fight against it."

"That's okay," Jon said. "Right now, we all have to get out of here!"

"No," Sasha said firmly. "Melantha and I live here. This is our home. We're not leaving."

"That angry mob out there is ready to lynch us!"

"Melantha and I will go out and talk to them. When they see she is set free, they will stop looking for you. The two of you can go back to the village after everything calms down."

"That doesn't sound like a good idea."

"I know my people. They will be happy to see that Melantha is well."

"My mother is very angry," Melantha said anxiously. "She may beat me, or force me to move out of her tent. She depended on the lizard to make a lot of money."

"We will talk with her as well," Sasha said. "If she doesn't want you to live with her any longer, we will find another place for you to stay. Trust me!"

"Okay," Melantha replied meekly.

Sasha took Melantha's hand, and the two of them walked to the center of the gypsy camp. Everyone stopped searching for the two men, and they gathered around them when they heard that Melantha was there.

"Tell them what happened," Sasha whispered to Melantha. "Tell them in your own words exactly what happened. Don't be afraid."

Melantha stood there for a moment and said nothing. Sasha began to think that she was just going to run away without saying a word. Then Melantha swallowed hard and said in a loud, clear voice, "Since I was a child, an evil being held me captive. It controlled my body and my mind. It lived on my back as a parasite, draining my life away from me and using me to deceive people with lies. It blinded me so that I lived in total darkness. Two men came into our camp today, not to rob or steal, but to rescue me and give me my life back. They showed me how King Tavon loves me and came to set me free. They got rid of the evil creature that imprisoned me. My eyes have now been opened and I can see!" She held up both of her hands high above her head, showing that both of her arms were bare except for a silver band on each wrist. "My chains are gone! I am free!"

The people in the camp were amazed by Melantha's transformation. They spent hours asking Sasha and Melantha how something so incredible could take place. Everyone hugged and kissed the two of them and wanted to know more about this King Tavon. Some of Sasha's friends built a bonfire, and with Melantha's permission, they burned all the fortune telling paraphernalia.

Calypso's heart remained hard, wicked and greedy. She dug up all the money she had buried in the woods and placed it in a satchel. Then she cursed and screamed at everyone in the camp one last time. A large nekron jumped on her back and she ran off into the darkness, never to be seen in the gypsy camp again.

When Jon and Traven saw the people hugging Melantha and Sasha, and smiling, they quietly walked back to Sugstal. The key would have to wait to be found another day.

CHAPTER 23

The Orphans' Ride

Tasca led seven of the orphans through the North Gate into Sugstal. They were all boys ranging from seven to ten years old. They bounced down the street and ran back and forth with boundless energy. They were very excited because they were about to go on a windship for the very first time. Litfim was there, as well as his older brother Storfim. Storfim looked just like Litfim, only he was a year older, a few inches taller, and his hair was just a bit darker. They came to the door of the Ansen's windship yard, and Tasca corralled them all together.

"Boys, I want you all to be on your best behavior," Tasca said to the orphans. "When you are on the windship, you must obey the captain's orders and do everything the crewmen tell you. If you don't, someone may get seriously hurt." Storfim stood in the back of the group behind his brother. He was pinching the back of his brother's neck just to annoy him.

"Stop it!" Litfim yelled, turning and slapping his brother's hand away. Storfim went from smiling deviously to trying to look innocent with his hands behind his back.

"Storfim, leave your brother alone!" Tasca scolded the boy. "What did I just say?" Storfim just looked at Tasca and shrugged his shoulders. "On the windship, you must do everything the captain and crew tell you. Is that clear?" Storfim nodded even though he did not really know what she was talking about. "Okay, let's go inside."

Tasca opened the door, and all seven boys tumbled into the small reception area.

Behind the counter, in the reception area, stood Nathan. He looked at all the boys and wondered why Ben kept inviting the orphans to take a ride on a windship. They could not stand still, and two of them kept talking and making rude noises. "Quiet!" Nathan shouted. When the room fell silent, Nathan said, "Welcome to the Sugstal Windship Yard. I am Nathan, the owner's son and the navigator. I'm the one who plots the course the windship takes and keeps track of where it is. My brother, Ben, is the captain. On the windship, he is the boss and everyone follows his orders. That means you must do everything he says, including wearing a life vest and always keeping your seatbelt firmly fastened. If you don't do what the captain says, you may fall overboard and drown!"

Toward the back of the group, Storfim was trying to make another boy laugh by mocking Nathan's speech. He crossed his eyes and opened and closed his mouth in a synchronization to Nathan's words. The other boy giggled. Tasca gave them both a stern look, and Storfim pretended to listen to Nathan again.

"Everyone follow me," Nathan said to the group. The boys followed Nathan through the door behind the counter into the large launch room, with its high, three-storied ceiling. A small windship sat on rails in the middle of this space. It said *Bluejay* on its side. All of Ansen's windships were named after birds of various colors. This was the smallest of his ships, very fast and nimble. Ben liked to use this ship when giving people from the village rides, because it was easy to handle with a smaller crew, and it was designed to only fly short distances. It had only one hull and one deck. In the middle of the deck were nine seats facing forward in three rows of three. The helm was near the stern, just behind the last row of passenger seats. Behind the wheel were three more seats for the crew. There was also a single seat near the bow for a crewman.

"Everyone must wear a lifejacket," Nathan shouted to the boys, holding up a stuffed vest. Each boy went over to a large bin and grabbed one of the vests. Nathan, and another man named Morlan, helped them put the vests on and tie the strap around their waists.

Some of the boys started getting nervous and bit at their fingernails. Litfim and Storfim ran back and forth between the bin and the windship, and appeared to be raring to go.

"Does everyone have a lifejacket on? Good! Follow me," Nathan said. He walked up a gangplank onto the deck of the *Bluejay*, and the boys cautiously followed him. Storfim ran up the plank and immediately began looking around at everything on the ship. Tasca walked up after him and told him to get back together with the rest of the group in the center of the windship.

"Everyone take a seat and belt yourself in," Nathan commanded. The boys all sat down and started strapping themselves in. Litfim and Storfim sat in the front row with an empty seat between them. Tasca sat in the middle seat in the back row. All the other boys filled the rest of the seats. "We are now going to place the windship on the ramp and take off," Nathan said in front of the group. "When the windship goes down the ramp, you will feel like your stomach is pushing you up and you are dropping down. That is completely natural. Don't be afraid. It's all part of the fun of being on a windship. Stay in your seats the whole time, unless the captain tells you otherwise. We don't want to see anyone get hurt."

Captain Ben came on board and looked at the boys and Tasca. He walked to where Nathan had been standing and said, "Welcome aboard the *Bluejay*. I'm Captain Bensareon. We are going to fly around the fjord this morning for about an hour, and then we will be coming right back here. Everyone has a lifejacket?" All the boys nodded. "Everyone is belted into their seat?" They all nodded again. "Good! Enjoy the ride."

The *Bluejay* was turned onto the rails of the launch ramp. After the crew went through a final checklist, Morlan shouted from the ground, "Clear for launch, Captain!"

"Clear for launch!" repeated the bows-man Herson.

"Clear for launch, sir!" shouted the sterns-man Einar.

"Launch the ship, Bersten," Ben said to the helmsman, taking the seat to the left of the wheel and strapping himself in. Nathan had already taken the seat to the right of the helmsman.

"Aye, aye, sir!" The helmsman threw a heavy lever, and the windship began moving slowly forward. A loud thud came from under the windship, and it began to move faster. All of a sudden, the front of the ship dropped down sharply, and the windship sped down the ramp. The grinding of wheels beneath the windship sounded like it was being ripped apart on both sides. All the boys began screaming. Then the bow of the ship came up again, and suddenly, all was silent except for the hum of the engines below deck. The *Bluejay* was airborne. It seemed to hover in place for a moment, and then it turned to the right and headed south over the fjord.

"Do it again!" one of the boys shouted. "Yeah! Do it again!" another one agreed.

The windship gently turned and followed the cliffs of the fjord. All the boys were amazed and smiling from ear to ear. Tasca was wishing she was on solid land and had the day off. She gripped the armrests of her chair as if her life depended on it.

"Give them a little excitement, Bersten," Ben said calmly.

"Aye, aye, sir," Bersten replied. The helmsman spun the wheel hard to port, and the bow of the windship suddenly dropped sharply and went plunging to the left. The boys felt their stomachs do the same kind of flip-flops they had done on the launch ramp, and they tightly gripped the armrests of the chairs. A collective "Whoa!" went up from the mouths of the orphans on the deck. The windship skimmed the surface of the fjord, and then it rose straight up to its original height. It spun around once slowly with its bow straight up in the air, and then it turned left again and dove back down toward the water.

Tasca felt like she was going to throw up her breakfast, but the boys seemed to be really enjoying the ride. After Bersten did one more spin and dive down into the fjord, Tasca looked back and said, "Can we please fly straight for a while?" Ben noticed she looked a bit pale, so he said to Bersten, "Ease the *Jay* down low across the water."

The windship dove gently until it was flying straight and level about ten feet above the water of the fjord. Down low and close to the sea, the windship felt like it was going much faster than when it was high over the mountain tops, because now the boys could see how quickly the rocks on the cliffs were passing by.

It was darker there, and all the boys looked frightened, except for Storfim. He suddenly felt very brave. Storfim unbuckled his seatbelt and ran forward toward the bow. At first, Herson did not notice him, because he was busy adjusting lines on the starboard side of the windship, but when he turned to go back to his post, he saw Storfim standing on the bow rail with his arms out above his head.

"I'm flying!" Storfim shouted leaning out over the front of the bow. "Look at me!" the boy said, looking back at his friends. As he turned his head, Storfim's foot slipped off the railing and he tumbled over the front of the windship. Herson ran and tried to grab him, but it was too late.

"Man overboard! Man overboard!" Herson shouted.

"Emergency landing on the fjord!" Ben shouted. "Hard alee, Bersten!"

"Aye, hard alee!" Bersten replied, as he threw the wheel over hard to starboard. The bow of the windship suddenly rose up, and it spun around quickly. The boys screamed and so did Tasca. Bersten threw the wheel hard to port. Then the windship came smashing down into the fjord, and a large wave came crashing over the bow. The boys in the two front rows of seats got soaked by icy, cold water. Ben and Nathan ran to the bow of the windship.

"Do you see him, Herson?" Ben asked peering out into the darkness at the bottom of the fjord.

Herson paused a moment, praying the boy was not dead. "Yes, over there!" There was Storfim floating in his life vest, shivering in the cold and coughing. Just then, a ray of sunlight fell on him as if the light came from Ehadreon itself.

"Slightly to port, Bersten!" Ben shouted to the helmsman.

"Aye, sir! Two degrees port!" Bersten shouted back.

Ben removed his boots and his heavy captain's jacket. He grabbed a long line that was lying on the deck for emergencies. He placed the large loop at the end of the rope over his head and left shoulder. When the windship came within twenty yards of Storfim, Ben dove into the icy waters toward the boy. He grabbed Storfim by the collar of his vest, and the crew on board began pulling in the line as quickly as they could. Nathan and Herson threw a boarding net over the side of the windship and they climbed down on to it. Ben pushed Storfim toward them, and they pulled him up on to the deck. Then they helped Ben climb out of the freezing water as well.

Bersten came running to the port side with woolen blankets. He had already given blankets to the boys who got soaked by the wave. Storfim's lips were blue, and he was shivering uncontrollably. Bersten helped him get his wet clothes off and wrapped him in several blankets.

Ben was shaking from the cold as well. He went to a locker at the back of the windship and found dry clothes. Then he went below deck into the ship's head and quickly changed.

"Is he all right?" Ben asked when he came back up on deck and put his uniform jacket back on. He looked over at Storfim. He was now sitting in Tasca's seat in the last row of chairs and drinking some warm soup out of a mug with both hands.

"Yes, sir! I think we got to him in time. We just need to keep him warm," Bersten said.

Storfim looked up at Ben. "Thanks for saving my life," he said through chattering teeth. "Someday, I'll have to pay you back."

Ben sat down nearby to put his boots back on. As he bent down, he suddenly had a vision of a much older Storfim riding a white horse and leading the other orphans into battle. When all seemed lost, and Ben was about to die, they came charging to his rescue with bright blue swords blazing in their hands.

The vision was so vivid and real. Ben did not notice Tasca standing nearby until she put her hand on his shoulder and said, "Thank you for rescuing Storfim. What you did was very brave."

"Well, I couldn't leave him in the fjord. Lady Elaine would never forgive me," Ben said with a smile, pulling on his second boot.

Tasca said, "Well, I just wanted to thank you anyway." Then she bent down and quickly kissed him on the cheek.

Ben blushed and raised his eyebrows. He thought, *Suddenly, all these beautiful, young women are kissing me, and I don't even understand why. Maybe Tasca is interested in me after all.*

Ben stood up and looked at all the boys sitting in the chairs on the deck, shaking from the cold and fear. Then he said, "Let's get home, Bersten. We don't want these boys to freeze to death."

"Aye, aye, sir!" Bersten replied, and he turned the windship toward the docks in Sugstal.

No one ever saw the tall woodsman, who was standing on deck, vanish into thin air.

CHAPTER 24

The Violet Sword

Sasha was carrying wood back to the fire at the western edge of the gypsy camp when she heard a shriek. She dropped the wood and ran back toward the campfire. There was Berk, covered in yellow-green dust, drunk and asleep on a chair. Elderly Hala was also there, trembling in fear and pointing at two large snakes under his seat. The twin snakes were each over ten feet long. They had been assigned to watch over the yellow-green key while Lacertus was away reporting to the Dragon. They were chained together so that they appeared to be one creature with two heads.

Sasha unsheathed her violet sword as she ran toward Hala and the snakes. "Get behind me, Hala!" she commanded the old lady. Hala obeyed by backing away. Sasha boldly stepped forward holding the sword with both hands.

"Do you think you can challenge both of us and win, little girl?" one of the snakes hissed.

"We have conquered mighty warriors far greater than you!" taunted the other snake.

The serpents moved closer to where Sasha was standing. They suddenly twisted in such a way that the large, black chain attached to their bodies came flying toward Sasha's head. She managed to duck and block the blow. The chain glanced off her sword, but it pushed Sasha sideways. She stepped back as far as she could and threw her sword toward the head of one of the serpents. It darted its head out of the way, and the blade flew harmlessly past it. The snakes drew closer

98

as the chain began to furiously whirl above their heads. Sasha's sword flew back into her hand. The snakes propelled the rotating chain toward Sasha. She ducked and rolled out of the way of the spinning menace. Once more, she threw her sword toward the snakes, and again they darted out of the path of the blade. The snakes moved toward her again, and the chain came smashing against Sasha's left side. It knocked her off her feet, and it knocked the wind out of her lungs. She groaned as she hit the ground. Her sword landed point down in the snow about ten feet away from her. The snakes moved in for the kill.

Suddenly, a bright blade came flying toward the snakes. It sliced through the side of one of the snake's heads, but it was not mortally wounded. A large woodsman bounded into the space between Sasha and the serpents, and their attention was now diverted to him. It was Anskar. As Anskar and the snakes engaged in battle, Sasha managed to get back up on her feet. She held her side where the chain had hit her. Her ribs ached terribly all across that side of her body. She pulled her sword out of the snow with her right hand.

The woodsman stepped back to where she was standing and said, "We must attack them together. Throw your sword when I throw mine . . . now!"

Both Sasha and Anskar threw their blades toward the serpents. The snakes quickly slithered down into a ditch in the ground with the chain flying after them. Anskar's sword came flying back around into his hand like a boomerang. Sasha's sword flew over the serpents and headed toward where Berk was slumped over in his chair, still fast asleep. Berk's jacket was hanging off the side of the chair. Inside his pocket was the yellow-green key. When Sasha's sword missed the snakes, it flew in an arc and sliced through Berk's pocket. As it passed through Berk's jacket, Sasha's sword melded with the key. Her blade flew back around and landed in the ground near where she and Anskar were standing. It was now shining with a brilliant, violet light, brighter than it had ever shone before. New, complex etchings radiated all the colors of the rainbow from the surface of the blade.

"No-ooo!" cried one of the snake heads. "Failure!" screamed its twin. "We are doomed!" both serpents hissed simultaneously.

Anskar pulled Sasha's sword from the ground, and holding the hilt toward her said, "Now daughter of the Highest, take your blade and send the serpents to where they belong!"

Sasha did as he commanded. She grabbed the sword, and it felt lighter and better-balanced in her hand. She threw it in a perfect arc toward the two snakes. They attempted to move out of the way of the blade, but it pierced both of their hearts at the same time. They vaporized in a brilliant, violet explosion. Then the blade gently circled around and landed perfectly in her hand.

Sasha stared at the sword in wonder. "This is not mine!" she said, shaking her head.

"But it *is* yours, Sasha. It is your destiny," Anskar said.

"What do you mean? What just happened here?" she asked.

"You are now the guardian of the violet key. No one can take it from you. It is yours to use for the good of the kingdom until you enter into your rest."

"No! Who am I that I should bear such a treasure? I'm no one! I'm nothing! I'm just a poor gypsy girl." Tears now began falling down her cheeks.

"You are a princess of the eternal house of Tavon, and his kingdom shall never end. He has chosen you to wield the key for his glory."

"No, please give it to someone else—someone more worthy of it," she said, holding her sword across her hands and offering it to Anskar.

"The Highest One never takes back the gifts he gives. Use it wisely!"

She winced in pain as she let down her sword. Holding her side, she sat down on a large rock nearby.

"Let me help you," Anskar said. He gently placed his hand on her side, and she felt the pain in her ribs fade away. Then he turned and began walking away with his sword in his hand.

"But I have so many questions," Sasha shouted after him.

Anskar turned for a moment and said, "When you need to know the answers, they will be given to you, but not a moment sooner." And he walked into the woods.

Meanwhile, a drunk, green and smelly Berk was still snoring away through everything that had just happened. After Anskar left, he opened his eyes for a moment and saw Hala smiling and standing by the fire. She had a knife in her hand, and she was paring an apple and eating it. He turned his head slightly and saw that Sasha was there as well. Then he blacked out again.

CHAPTER 25

The Dissatisfied Passenger

Ben was eager to get back home. He never liked it when they flew the circuit from Sugstal to Rothal to Babbelar and home again, because many of the Corasarian passengers were difficult to please, but it always paid well. The crew was now preparing to launch the *White Eagle* from the ramp in the capital city of Babbelar. They should have already been in the air, but they were delayed by two of the passengers. A man and his wife were complaining about their accommodations and refusing to get on board the windship. He looked like a big, warty toad, and she looked like a round, green ball holding a large frog. They both had large, yellow-green chains across their shoulders. It was Arboron and his wife, Histrionicah. A thin, old man in a worn, black suit stood behind them next to their luggage. He was their manservant.

"I must have a room all to myself," the pale, round woman insisted. "I cannot possibly sit for hours with strangers crammed into a tiny, little cabin!" She stuck her nose in the air, looked away from Ben, and patted the back of her thick, green hair with her bejeweled hand.

"I'm sorry, ma'am, but there *are* no other cabins," Ben said, trying to be as patient as possible.

"Surely there must be more than one room on this stupid thing!" she sneered. The lap-frog in her arms appeared to be smiling.

"There is only one cabin for those who are traveling with us, ma'am," Ben explained.

"Well, can't I stay up on top? Why do I have to go down into the stinking belly of this thing?" she asked, as she waved her hand toward the windship. As she moved her arm, Ben noticed the thick, rusty, yellow-green shackle around her wrist. Diamonds had somehow been attached to it, but they could not hide its unsightly appearance.

"For your own safety, ma'am, you need to stay below deck. We wouldn't want you to get hurt or fall off the deck when we are hundreds of feet in the air," Ben explained.

"Where does your crew stay?" she demanded harshly. Arboron, who was standing next to her, groaned out loud and he whispered, "Maybe it wouldn't be so bad if she fell off the deck hundreds of feet in the air."

"They fly the windship from the deck and the pilothouse," Ben said, finding it very difficult to not sound annoyed.

"How about I stay in this pilothouse thing?" she whined.

"No, only the crew are allowed in there." Actually, only the crew who were granted permission from the captain were allowed on the bridge, but Ben was not about to try to explain that to her. He tried to set aside the fact that she just insulted his authority as captain by inviting herself onto his bridge.

"You are not pleasing me, *captain*!" she screamed. "My husband and I are very important and influential people! You don't want to find yourself at odds with us!"

"We are leaving right now, ma'am! If you don't feel comfortable coming on board, you're welcome to stay here!" Ben could feel the anger rising up inside him, and he hated the experience. He turned away from them and went on board his ship.

"We will not accept being treated so rudely, captain!" she screamed at his back. "My husband has the *best* lawyers on retainer! We will *sue* you!"

Then she turned her wrath on her husband. "Arboron, how can you just stand there and allow him to treat me this way?" She suddenly started crying crocodile tears.

Arboron rolled his eyes and shook his head. Then he climbed on board and walked over to where Ben was standing on deck. He reached into his pocket and leaning in toward Ben, he whispered,

"Look captain, can't we come to some sort of agreement here?" He pushed a fist full of paper money into Ben's front pocket.

Ben pulled the money out of his pocket and held it out to Arboron. "I'm sorry sir, but there is only one cabin where passengers can stay on this ship. I can't change that fact."

"But surely there must be room for . . . exceptions," Arboron mumbled, as he waved his hands in front of him as if he was trying to materialize something out of thin air.

Ben grabbed Arboron's hand and pressed the money into it. Then he said, "You have five minutes, sir, to decide whether you would like to come on board. If you are not below deck by then, we will leave without you." Then he started giving orders to the crew up in the rigging.

"You will give us a full refund, then," Arboron insisted, but Ben had walked away and was no longer listening. "You know, the customer always comes first!" he said only to himself.

Nathan walked over to him and said, "We are about to depart, sir. Please do not disturb the captain during our final preparations. We ask you to take your seat below or disembark!"

Arboron cursed under his breath and went down to his wife. "Well, did he give us the pilothouse?" she said indignantly, with her stubby arms folded across her chest. She was no longer crying her false tears.

"Ah . . . no. Histrionicah . . . dearest . . . there is no other cabin. We just have to do what they say." He said this looking away from her toward the windship. He could not look her in the eye. He knew she would throw a fit and maybe even become violent, but he knew it was best to get it over with and tell her the truth.

"If you think I'm going to get on that stinking boat, you are totally out of your stinking mind!" she screamed, as she stamped her foot and punched him hard in the chest. Then she commanded her servant to take her bags, and she stomped out of the windship yard. She expected her husband to follow her out, but he just watched her walk away. The thought of passing up a potentially large profit in Sugstal caused him to hesitate for just a moment. After all, he did love his wealth much more than his wife.

Nearby sat the large toad that always accompanied Arboron everywhere he went. Wartvox knew that he had to get Arboron on the windship to complete the Dragon's plan. So he said, "I've been dying to get away from that witch for ages. Now's my chance to have peace and be free of her. It would show her if I just got on board and left her behind. Yeah, what a great idea!"

As usual, Arboron thought the toad's words were his own thoughts. So he said, "Yeah, I'll show her!" and he grabbed his bag and climbed on board the windship just before it was moved over to the launch ramp. As he sat down in the passenger cabin with the other passengers, he smiled and said, "This trip is going to be even better than I thought!" He did not realize he was just repeating the words of the large toad beneath his seat.

CHAPTER 26

The Lost Key

Stang was making his usual rounds of the camp when he heard shouts and a scream. The noises came from one of the widow's wagons on the western edge of the camp. As Stang ran in that direction, he heard Berk yelling, "It's mine, lady! Where'd you put it? I want it back!"

A feeble, high pitched voice cried, "I don't have it! Please leave me alone!" Stang recognized the voice belonged to little old Hala. He heard the sickening sound of several blows and a body falling to the floor of a wagon. He bounded up the steps of Hala's wagon and he saw the door was ajar. When he looked inside, he saw big, hairy Berk leaning over Hala's frail form with a large, green chain in his hands. The chain was also now attached to his neck. Blood was splattered all over Berk's face and clothes. His whole body was also covered in yellow-green dust.

"What have you done now, you stupid idiot?" Stang snarled through clenched teeth.

Berk looked up at Stang and said, "Nothin', boss. I was just looking for somethin' and I thought maybe the old lady had it."

Stang knelt down next to the tiny body of Hala and put his hand on her neck, hoping to feel a pulse. She showed no signs of life.

Stang stood up again and growled, "What was it you were looking for, Berk?"

"Nothin' important," Berk mumbled.

"You beat a little old lady to death for *'nothing?'* You're looking very green, Berk! It wouldn't happen to be a key now, would it?"

"No! Of course not, boss." Berk clutched at the torn pocket of his jacket.

"Don't lie to me, Berk, or I'll kill you right now!"

"Maybe," Berk said looking down at the floor. "Maybe . . . but she stole it from me!"

"And you stole it from my wagon, Berk!"

Berk knew he was in big trouble, so he jumped on top of Stang and tried to overpower him. Stang stepped aside and used the momentum of Berk's body to throw him out of the door of the wagon. Berk tumbled down the steps and fell on the ground. He groaned as pain shot through his spine and out to all parts of his body. He scrambled to his feet and started running toward the woods. Berk was not very intelligent, but he knew that he would lose if he tried to take on Stang in a fight. Stang ran after him.

They ran all the way through the woods, down the mountainside for about two miles to the South Road. Berk ran for his life. Stang ran to take the life of a murderer. Berk stumbled and fell as he ran across the road, so Stang slowed to a walking pace since they were both out of breath. Berk managed to get back up on his feet, and he kept stumbling eastward toward the cliffs. Stang followed him at the same walking pace until Berk finally came close to the edge of the rockface dropping far down into the fjord.

"It was just an accident, boss, really!" Berk pleaded standing near the ledge.

"What was an accident, Berk? You taking the key from me? Or you killing a defenseless, old woman?" Stang moved closer. He was not going to allow Berk to escape.

"Uh . . . both! I didn't really mean to do it!" Berk tried to back away from Stang, but every step just brought him closer to the edge of the cliff.

"Where is the key now, Berk?"

"I don't know. I thought the old lady had it, really!" Berk was in tears now. He had often seen how ruthless Stang could be toward those who had crossed him. He was truly frightened.

"She's not all green like you, Berk. So I doubt she took it!"

"She must have! She was the only one around when I fell asleep by the fire. She cut it out of my pocket!"

"Hala was not a thief like you, Berk! Someone else must have been there."

Suddenly Berk remembered something, and a look of surprise came over his face. "*She* was there, too!" As he said this, he dropped the green chain he was holding in his hand. Since the chain was also attached to his neck, dropping it threw his head forward. He started leaning backwards to compensate for the chain's weight. Then he realized he was out of balance and tipping backwards. His feet were slipping out from under him on the edge of the cliff. He desperately tried to regain his balance. Then terror filled his heart as he suddenly found himself plummeting hundreds of feet, headfirst into the fjord.

Stang jumped forward in a vain attempt to grab Berk's jacket and rescue him, but he had already slipped over the edge. "She *who*, Berk?" he shouted to the mangled body on the rocks far below. "Who is *she*?"

CHAPTER 27

The Rude Customer

Sasha walked to work that morning with a warmth in her heart that overflowed onto her beautiful face. As she came into the *White Stallion* to begin work for the day, she was glowing and so was the violet sword on her back. She greeted her boss, Magnus, with a winsome smile. "Good morning, sir."

"Good morning, Sasha. You're looking even more charming than ever! Why all the smiles? Did something good happen yesterday?" Magnus asked.

"Yes, I guess you could say that," she said spinning around to talk to him. She smiled brightly, turned around again and skipped to the kitchen to put her apron on. She put a broad smile on Magnus' face as well. He felt like a proud father, even though he was not really her father. It warmed his own heart to see her so happy. He started humming a joyful song to himself that he had heard sung at the prayerhouse.

Later that day, Arboron followed the other passengers off the windship and onto the dock at Sugstal. He was still smiling from warty ear to warty ear at the thought of spending time away from his wife. Yet he felt winded by the time he climbed up the steps to the windship yard, so his positive mood had faded away by the time he reached the top of the stairs. He grumpily asked a man on High Street where he could get a meal, and the man pointed to the *White Stallion* down the street.

It was now lunch time, and as usual, the *White Stallion* was full of people—eating, telling stories and laughing. Magnus and his staff had their hands full as always. The place was filled with villagers enjoying life, and at the center of it all was a very hardworking Sasha.

Arboron came in and sat down at a table in the corner. He was feeling really tired and cranky now. Because of his obesity, the walk up the stairs with his luggage had drained all the energy out of his body. As he began looking over the menu, he grumbled, "What horribly bland food this is. They don't even have a decent wine cellar. Their prices are so low the food must be horrendous! Well, what can you expect when you're out in the middle of the sticks."

Sasha came over to Arboron's table. At first, she felt uncomfortable when she saw the many pustules and warts on his frog-shaped head, but she still smiled at him and said, "What can I get for you, sir?"

"Whatever happens to be edible on this menu," he growled, tossing the menu aside.

"Would you like for me to recommend something?" she said politely. When he just sat there scowling at her, she said, "The venison pie is very good today."

"Okay, get me that," he mumbled, with an expression of disgust across his pockmarked, warty face. "I hope it doesn't poison me. And bring me an ale if it doesn't taste like dishwater!"

Sasha found herself wishing that someone else was serving this customer. She felt like he had brought a negative spirit into the *White Stallion*. Even though she did not see it, a large, evil toad sat under Arboron's table.

Arboron watched her walk back to the kitchen, not because he thought she was pretty, but because he was evaluating her worth. Like most Corasarians, Arboron felt that a person's value was based on the cost of their wardrobes, the size of their houses, the number of their servants, and the wealth of their fields. This girl was dressed in old, worn-out shoes and a tattered dress. Her apron was dirty and she was even sweating! She was working as a waitress in a backwater village, and she even looked like a penniless gypsy! His servants were dressed better than she was, so she must be beneath them in value— the lowest of the low. He concluded that she must own nothing of real worth. He found nothing attractive about this girl. Actually, he despised her and her poverty.

When Sasha brought the venison pie and ale over to his table, Arboron said, "It's about time! A man could die of hunger before he got served in this stinking place!"

Several large farmers at a neighboring table looked over at Arboron and shook their heads.

"Doing my best, sir!" Sasha said, juggling several plates as she placed the pie in front of him. "One of our waitresses is not feeling well today."

"They should hire more staff here," he mumbled. "They're losing customers by making them wait. These backwater peasants don't even know how to run an efficient business."

When Arboron finished his meal, Sasha came over to his table and asked, "Would you like anything else, sir?"

"No, just tell me what I owe you for this foul garbage!" he said angrily pushing his plate aside.

Sasha said, "Please pay Magnus, the owner, at the door on your way out."

"I would like to give you a tip, young lady," Arboron said sternly.

"Thank you, you can just leave it on the table," Sasha said, about to turn away.

"No, you're not worthy of my *money*, I want to give you some *advice*. I wanted to tell you that if you just thought positive thoughts instead of negative ones, you would no longer have to live in poverty and dress in those filthy rags," he said looking her up and down. "You know, you could almost look attractive if you got yourself some nice clothes and you stopped working in a horrible place like this!"

The four large farmers, sitting at a neighboring table, suddenly stood up when they heard Arboron's comments to Sasha. They surrounded Arboron, and they all appeared to be very angry and incredibly muscular. One of them grabbed Arboron's collar in his huge fist, and he lifted him out of his chair with one arm. Looking him squarely in the eyes, he said, "We don't speak that way to our ladies here, toad face! If I were you, I would apologize to her before I rip your warty, little nose off!"

"Sorry," Arboron meekly croaked. He was wheezing and gasping for air.

"I don't think she heard you, frog breath!" the farmer growled.

"Sorry, Miss!" he said again a little louder, darting his eyes in Sasha's direction. The farmer dropped him, and he slumped down on to the floor in a heap.

All four of the men gave Arboron stern looks as they left the room. "Let us know if you have any more problems, Miss," a second farmer said as they all tipped their hats to Sasha.

"Thanks, boys!" she said as they all walked by.

"Our pleasure, Sasha!" said a third farmer.

She looked over at Arboron, holding his throat and lying limply on the floor. "Thanks for the advice," she said. "I'm feeling more positive already!" She winked at him, smiled and walked back to the kitchen.

Under the table sat the large toad that followed Arboron everywhere he went. Wartvox was laughing.

CHAPTER 28

The White Light

When Berk opened his eyes, he found himself standing in a vast, open area that was cold and dark. The darkness felt like it was tangible—as if it had physical form and substance. The surface under his feet was dark gray, hard, and perfectly flat. The only thing he could see for miles around was a white light, far off in the distance. He felt incredibly alone and isolated, and it filled him with a sense of desperate terror.

"Where am I?" he said out loud. The last thing he could remember was falling from the cliff. He realized he must have died. He had heard stories about people who had passed away for a few moments and then come back to life again. They always mentioned seeing a bright light in front of them and being drawn to that light. That must be what was happening to him now. He decided to start running toward the light. It was better than sitting all alone in that dark, terrible place.

He soon passed under an immense, stone archway. It stretched for thousands of yards across. At the top, huge letters were etched into the rocks. Even though Berk could not read very well, he understood what was written there. It read: The Wide Gate to the Broad Way. He thought he must be heading in the right direction. Berk kept running toward the light, and it became larger and brighter. He began to also see other people running toward the light. It gave him a little comfort to know that he was not the only one there.

Soon he came up to a large crowd of millions of people, and he could run no further. The crowd stretched out for as far as he could see in every direction. He noticed that everyone around him in the crowd was horribly deformed in some way. Some were missing limbs or parts of their faces. Others were horribly burned or marred. Others just looked incredibly twisted and ugly.

"So is this the entrance to paradise?" Berk asked hopefully to no one in particular.

"Paradise?" a man standing next to him exclaimed. "You're in the wrong line, mister!" The man had no ears and a vicious scar across his forehead. "This here is the queue to appear before the Judge."

"But there's that bright, white light over there!" Berk said as he pointed to it.

"That's what they call The Great White Throne," a deformed hag with no teeth cackled. "That's where the Judge sits."

"Who's the Judge?" Berk asked.

"Some people are calling him Tavon. Others are calling him Joshua or something like it," the hag said. When she said the name *Tavon,* Berk felt very guilty. He had often heard people talk about Tavon, but he had never really paid much attention to what they said. Now he was wishing he had taken the time to listen.

As Berk looked around, he saw a cloud of thick black smoke billowing out of a deep chasm far to the left of the throne. The smoke filled all the sky and made the entire area incredibly dark. An eerie, roaring sound also filled the air. It sounded like thousands of pieces of wood being hit together and an incredibly loud beehive. Berk did not understand what it was, so he asked, "What's all that noise?"

"It's the sound of utter and complete despair," the earless man answered, "the sound of countless thousands weeping and gnashing their teeth."

"But why should anyone be upset? We all go to paradise anyway, right?" Berk asked desperately. He was getting upset himself now.

"Haaa!" the hag laughed. "He thinks we all go to paradise, isn't that sweet?" she said to the earless man, and pointing to Berk with her thumb.

Berk began to really become worried now. So he said, "But the Judge must show some pity—some mercy!"

"He's ruthless!" the hag hissed in Berk's face. "He has no pity! When he asks you a question, you'd better have the right answer or you're doomed!"

"What kind of questions does he ask?" Berk shrieked. He was very frightened now and showing it.

"We heard he only asks one question: 'How did you treat orphans and widows?'" the earless man said.

"I should be okay, then," the hag said proudly. "*I am* a widow. I should know. I killed my nasty husband myself!" She cackled with laughter.

Someone further up in the crowd shouted, "Alas, he's treating us the same way we treated others!"

Berk's heart filled with dread as he remembered how he had mistreated young Litfim and how he took innocent Hala's life. He looked down at his twisted hands, and he saw several heavy chains attached his wrists. The largest of the chains was yellow green. It felt immensely heavy now. He realized that he was dreadfully guilty, and his guilt was now overwhelming his soul like a huge millstone around his neck. Filled with deep despair, Berk screamed out loud in terror. He started running away from the Throne toward the smoke billowing out of the Abyss. He decided that it would better for him to hurl himself into the Abyss than to face the one seated on the Great White Throne—so that is exactly what he did, and so did many others.

CHAPTER 29

The Foolproof Plan

It was the middle of the night, and the lizard, Lacertus, was talking to Arboron's toad, Wartvox, in an alley next to the *Wayside Inn* in Sugstal. Lacertus was now trying to accomplish the second stage of the plan. He had no idea that the key had melded with Sasha's sword, nor did he know that the twin snakes guarding it had been defeated.

"You must get him to the South Wood tomorrow morning," Lacertus hissed.

"Ribbit! Gree-dee! He will be there," the toad promised.

"It will be easy to get the key into his hands. I've trained the fool who has the key now to love his ale. I'll just make sure he is blind drunk tomorrow. Then your fool can easily steal it from him," Lacertus explained.

"The plan is *foolproof* then! Ribbit! Gree-dee!" The toad laughed at his own pun. Lacertus laughed as well. "He will be blind drunk so we can rob him blind! Gree-dee! Gree-dee!" Wartvox laughed again.

Lacertus laughed so hard he fell over on his side—the side with the chain attached to it. Then he remembered the plan was an order given to him by the Dragon. He stopped laughing and said, "Stop it! This is serious, Wartvox! If we fail, the consequences will be extremely painful for both of us!"

"How can we fail with the twin serpents guarding the key?" the toad asked.

The lizard's lips curled up into a diabolical smile. "You're right, my warty friend! The plan *is* foolproof!" Lacertus agreed, and they both laughed some more.

*   *   *   *   *

The next morning, Arboron decided he did not want to get out of bed. The voice in his head kept telling him he should get up and find the forest that will bring him a fortune, but he just did not feel like it. His flabby body was telling him to roll over and sleep some more, so that is exactly what he did.

By ten o'clock in the morning, Lacertus was getting anxious and angry. *Wartvox had promised the fool would be on his way to the woods by now,* he thought. Lacertus snuck out of his hiding place near the alley, and he scurried into a back window of the *Wayside Inn*. He did not like running the risk of being seen in the daylight in this part of the village. There were far too many of those loyal to his Enemy here. He scurried up the back stairs toward Arboron's room, trying to stay in whatever shadows he could find. As he got to the second floor, two of Ebesian's students came out into the hallway. Landron and Gransen were talking about the key. Lacertus quickly darted under a table in the hallway, and like a chameleon, he changed his colors to blend into the background around him.

"Ebus says we should find it in the next day or so," Landron said as he closed the door to their room.

"Then there are only six to go!" Gransen responded. "It's all pretty exciting!"

While Gransen headed for the main stairway, Landron stopped for a moment. He turned to look down the opposite end of the hallway. He sensed that something did not seem right, but he did not see anything unusual, so he turned to join his friend on the staircase.

When the two students left, Lacertus came out from under the table and he slipped into Arboron's room that was right next to theirs. From listening to the students' conversation, he knew that he needed to act fast, and he became even more irate with Wartvox. As he entered the room, he saw Arboron asleep in the bed and the large toad asleep at the foot of it. He punched Wartvox in the head and the toad woke up.

"Why are you sleeping, wart-face?" Lacertus hissed as he punched the toad again. "Why isn't the fool on the way to the woods?"

"Ribbit! Gree-dee! I couldn't get him out of bed. I tried all morning. Croak! It's not my fault."

"How is it not your fault, dragon's fodder?"

"This is what happens when we give them too many vices. He's so fat and lazy, even greed does not motivate him at times! Perhaps we should have chosen someone else," Wartvox explained.

Lacertus understood the problem. He had experienced the same situation many times before. "It's so hard to know how much vice and virtue is needed in a victim to get them to do what you want them to do. Too much vice and they become useless or die too quickly. Too much virtue and they cannot be controlled. Since greed will not motivate him, now we must use fear!"

"I understand," the toad croaked. He hopped over to the bed where Arboron was sleeping. He started filling Arboron's dreams with images of his barns burning, his wife divorcing him and glee-fully taking everything that he owned, and being thrown into a cold, dark debtor's prison with no hope of ever getting out.

Arboron woke up screaming. He felt like he was about to have a heart attack. Then he realized it was all just a nightmare. He quickly got out of bed and put his clothes on. He had important business to attend to. A forest with his name on it was waiting for him out there.

CHAPTER 30

The Ransacked Wagon

When the news of Hala's death spread throughout the camp, some of the gypsies ran over to Hala's wagon with sacks in their hands. The looting started quickly, and it was over in just minutes. They took everything the widow owned, whether or not it was nailed down. Her clothes, food, and blankets vanished first. Then they stole her dishes, silverware, pots and pans. The latecomers took her old shoes and knickknacks. The men disassembled the wagon so quickly, in only moments it was just a broken, wheel-less box on the ground.

Sasha came out of her wagon when she heard the sound of banging and yelling next door. She saw two women arguing over Hala's underwear. They ended up tearing her bloomers in half. Three men were taking an ax to the wagon, breaking off the lanterns, shutters and wheels. Another man was trying to remove the door. Two others were carrying the cast iron stove off to their tent. Hala's granddaughter, Mara, knelt nearby, weeping bitterly with her hands over her face. Mara was the same age as Sasha, and a very close friend.

"What are you all doing?" Sasha shouted running down the steps of her wagon. "You can't do this! It's wrong!"

"It's the gypsy way, lass!" a big, middle-aged woman shouted over a stack of plates and cups. "She ain't using it anymore where she's gone!"

Sasha could not believe her eyes. She slowly walked over to what was left of Hala's wagon and looked inside. Everything had been stripped bare. The only things left were a broken clay pot and a book thrown carelessly on the floorboards. She gently picked up the book and carefully straightened out its wrinkled pages. Inside was a picture of Hala with Mara. They had taken all the meager belongings of a poor old widow, and left behind her most prized possession—her Lorebook. Sasha held the book close to her chest and wept.

Sasha ran over to Mara and took her by the hand. Then, still holding the Lorebook, Sasha lead Mara over to the bell hanging on a post at the center of the camp. She started ringing the bell furiously. The people in the gypsy camp started gathering around her, wondering what was the matter, because the bell was only rung on very important occasions. When almost everyone appeared to be there, Sasha stood up on a crate to address the crowd.

"Today, you have ransacked the wagon of a poor, dead widow, who isn't even buried yet!" Sasha shouted. "Hala had *one* nice dress, and now you have denied her the opportunity to be buried in it! Everything in that wagon should have gone to her granddaughter, Mara, but you selfish thugs stole it all for yourselves! You always talk about how horribly selfish the rich people in the city across the fjord are. You gossip about how the people in the village take advantage of you, and how they look down on you for being gypsies. Well, the people in Sugstal are right! You are *all* criminals and thieves! You should all be ashamed of yourselves, every last one of you who robbed Hala's wagon! I'm ashamed to even say you are my people! If you want food in the future, it's not going to come from *me!* You're just going to have to steal it, just like you do everything else!"

Sasha then marched through the crowd back to her wagon with tears running down her face. She tried to make sure that she made eye contact with everyone, but they all looked down at the ground as she walked by. Only Stang met her glance with a proud smile, and he had not taken anything from Hala's wagon. The people had never seen her angry before, and it scared all of them for they knew it was righteous anger. They felt especially guilty when they remembered how often Sasha had generously given them food. How would they survive if Sasha stopped being so benevolent?

As a result of Sasha's impassioned speech, people began leaving all the things they had taken from Hala outside Mara's door. Even the pieces of the wagon, like the boards, lanterns and wheels were left there. Each of the women would mumble an apology to Mara, and the men would tip their hats and bow to her. The woman who had taken Hala's best dress came with tears running down her face, with the dress carefully folded and a bouquet of flowers placed on top of it. When it was all over, there were twice as many things given to Mara as had been taken from Hala's wagon. Even people who had not taken anything gave her something from their own possessions. The steps of Sasha's wagon were also covered in flowers and vegetables. No one wanted Sasha to stop being generous.

CHAPTER 31

The Orange Princess

As Arboron walked out of the front doors of the *Wayside Inn*, Lacertus scurried down the back staircase and out of a window. Then he ran through the back alleyways to a crack in the southern wall, and onto the gypsy's camp. Wartvox waited until he knew Arboron was clear of the building. Then he was going to follow him in the shadows and coax him toward the South Woods.

At least that was the plan. Just as Wartvox left the room, Jon and Traven came out of the room across the hallway. The toad scrambled for the back stairs, hoping his camouflage had sufficiently concealed his presence, but before he could reach the back stairway, he felt the sting of Traven's blade. When Jon's blade ran through his heart, the toad vanished in a cloud of black smoke and he was gone.

"I knew something wasn't right last night," Traven said to Jon. "There was just something strange about that Corasarian who checked in yesterday."

"I think all Corasarians are strange!" Jon said. "We must be very close to finding the key. The enemy appears to be very interested in our activities."

Back out on the street, Arboron wandered around in circles, trying to decide where he should go next. Usually he was so decisive. Now the voice inside his head that always guided him to profitable ventures seemed to be silent. He began looking for someone to point him in the right direction.

Just then, Princess Gwynneth came strolling down High Street toward him. As usual, she was dressed like she was going to attend a ball. She was wearing a very expensive orange gown, lined with gold trim around the waist and ermine fur around the collar. Matching orange gloves with pearl buttons went up to her elbows. They covered the orange shackles and chain bound to her wrists. A large, orange, circular hat sat on top of her abundant, dark curls. A large peacock feather stuck out of her hat, and it bounced up and down as she strutted down the street. Even with all of her finery she was still quite unattractive, because she unfortunately had a silly disposition and a homely face. Her mouth and chin were too small, her nose was too large, and her eyes were set too close together. Her mind could only handle simple ideas, and it often caused her to jump to the wrong conclusions. She was the product of an aristocratic pedigree—a family tree where cousins married and mated far too often. Yet she truly believed she was smart and beautiful, because when she was growing up, they always told her so.

When Arboron saw Gwynneth, he thought that she was the most beautiful woman he had ever seen in his life. Here was someone who had wealth and good breeding. Here was someone who had looks *and* money! He was certain that she must come from an aristocratic family. He decided that he had to meet her, so he walked over to her as she was browsing at a shop window.

"Excuse me! I am Sir Arboron, chairman of the Western Forestry Guild," he said to her bowing and tipping his hat. "I wonder if you might be able to help me. I am supposed to meet someone for a business opportunity, but I am afraid I am lost."

"I am Princess Gwynneth of the royal house of Payton," she said holding out her gloved hand.

Arboron took her hand and kissed it. "So wonderful to meet you, your majesty. I knew the moment I saw you that you must be someone of noble birth. You have such a stately bearing and magnificent beauty." Gwynneth smiled and blushed at the compliment. "May I buy you lunch? It would be a great help to me if I could bend your pretty, little ear for a few moments. A cup of tea, perhaps?" Arboron held up his right hand and rubbed his fingers together as he extended the invitation. Money was always the first thing on his mind, even when he had inappropriate thoughts about a woman who was not his wife.

"Sure!" Gwynneth said enthusiastically. Finally, someone was treating her the way she deserved to be treated. "I was just on my way to the tea shop now."

Arboron and Gwynneth sat down at a small table by the window in *Dowagah's Tea Shop*. They ordered tea, scones, and cucumber sandwiches. A few other women sat at the other tables in pairs, quietly chatting. Arboron was the only man in the shop. As they chatted, he found that Gwynneth spoke as if she had lived in the area for quite some time. She described all that the village shops had to offer in vivid detail, because she had spent all of her time over the last few days shopping. She also talked about her close relationship with a local loremaster and his students. After some small talk about how cold the weather always is in Sugstal, Arboron got around to talking about what was really on his mind.

"You sound like you really know this area very well. I am here to buy a forest. Would you happen to know of any wooded acreage for sale near the village?" he asked.

"The only woods I know of are north, near the orphanage." Gwynneth had only been in Sugstal for a few days. The only time she had ever left the village was when she had wandered toward the orphanage one day trying to find Ebesian's students. They had treated her politely, but they did not include her in any of their meetings with the loremaster. Because of her naive optimism, she really did not notice that they had left her out.

"Does the orphanage own all of the trees?" Arboron asked.

"Oh yes! Just the other day I heard the headmistress say, 'We are so blessed to live here in a beautiful, one-hundred-acre forest.'" Gwynneth did hear Lady Elaine say this as she prayed with the children before they had their lunch.

"What does this forest look like?" he asked, extremely interested in hearing what she had to say. He thought that a one-hundred-acre forest was a very rare find, because most of the wooded land in his own country had been stripped bare of vegetation. He knew this to be a fact, because most of the trees had been harvested on his orders.

"Oh, the trees are beautiful and very old. Most of the trees are huge! If you could buy that wood, you'd have the most magnificent forest in Spysar!" she said with deep conviction, slowly nodding her head.

Arboron thought, *Here is a fine intelligent young woman, who really knows the area and has an appreciation of the finer things in life. This must be the forest I am looking for. My positive thoughts are leading me to greater prosperity!* To Gwynneth, he said, "How would I find this orphanage?"

"Oh, just go out of the North Gate of the village. You can't miss it!" she said sipping the last of her tea.

CHAPTER 32

The Revealed Secret

When Lacertus scurried into the gypsy camp that afternoon, he immediately started looking for the twin serpents, Berk, and the key, but all four were nowhere to be found. They all appeared to have vanished into thin air. The green dust trail from the key came to an end near the campfire pit on the western end of the camp. There, as he began to panic at the thought that the key was now in the hands of his enemy, he tried to think of more positive scenarios as to what might have happened.

First, he thought, *Maybe someone took the key from Berk and the snakes were now with that person instead. No, that can't be. There would be a green trail for me to follow to the new fool. The trail just seemed to end by the campfire. I've never seen that happen before!*

Next, he thought, *Maybe Berk died and they buried the key with him where the trail ends.*

Lacertus anxiously scurried all around the area by the campfire pit, but he could find no signs of recent digging. He dug a deep hole in the dirt at the end of the green trail and he still found nothing. No bodies or keys were hidden there.

The fools wouldn't bury Berk by the fire pit, he reasoned. *They don't like dead things near their children or their food. The Twins would also still be somewhere close by if the key had been buried here. They would not leave it unguarded.*

Lacertus began to realize that the key must be in the possession of someone loyal to Tavon, because it must have fully changed into

126

its violet form. It was the only explanation for why the green trail ended so abruptly. That meant that the twin snakes must have been dispatched by the enemy as well, because they would not have given it up without a fight. Yet who had been powerful enough to overcome the Twins?

Lacertus decided to search the gypsy camp for those loyal to Tavon. He would start with Sasha, since she seemed to be the greatest threat to his cause. If he did not find the key among the gypsies, then one of Ebesian's students had to have it. At that thought, he totally lost control of himself. He shouted curses and profanities and beat the ground with the thick, black chain attached to his body until he was totally exhausted.

Lacertus lay on his back, completely spent and out of breath from his fit of rage. When he finally regained his composure, he rolled over onto his belly and he began to think reasonably again. That positive thinking nonsense might have worked when it came to manipulating his victims, but he was not so stupid as to believe that it really worked. There was no other explanation for what had happened and he had to accept it. Even though the thought filled him with tremendous fear and anxiety, he decided to find out if Berk was dead and what agent of the Enemy had taken the key. He did not care about trying to find the twin snakes now. They would have to pay for their failure one way or another. He just hoped that he would not experience their fate as soon as they did.

*   *   *   *   *

Sasha sat in a wooden chair beside her wagon weeping and wiping her eyes with a handkerchief. All of the other women in the camp were also crying and hugging each other or their children. The men stood around them looking solemn and grim. A narrow casket containing Hala's body rested on the ground in the center of the group. "I'm so sorry, lass!" everyone was saying to Mara and Sasha as they tried to console them.

Stang came across the clearing, and he sat down in a chair beside Sasha. She looked at him through her tear-stained eyes, and he seemed to be less intimidating. He almost appeared to be friendly. He leaned forward in his chair, resting his elbows on his knees, and folded his hands together. For a moment, Sasha thought he was going to pray with her, but instead he spoke to her.

"I want you to know that I caught the person who did this, and justice has been served," he said to her in a low voice.

She suddenly became afraid of him again. "What did you *do*, sir?" she whispered with a wide-eyed expression on her face.

"I didn't *do* anything," Stang said quietly. "The fool fell. I even tried to save him, but I didn't get to him in time."

She studied his face for a moment. He seemed to be telling the truth. "Sir, why are you telling me this?"

"Because I want you to know that even though I was not able to protect Hala, you are in safe hands. I will be watching out for you."

"I didn't know that I was in danger," she whispered, very concerned now.

"All I know is that whoever possesses the object dies. If I were you, I would get rid of it as soon as possible. Understand?" he said looking straight into her eyes.

Sasha did not say anything. She did not know if he was making a threat or just telling her to be prudent. The fact that she did not lie and say, "I don't know what you're talking about" told him that she did in fact have the key. He had guessed correctly. She was the one who had been with Berk and Hala when the key went missing.

As he got up and walked away, Sasha realized that Stang now knew that she had the key, and she was not sure she could trust him. She began to see that being the guardian of the Murastan would not be an easy task. In fact, it might demand all that she had—even her life.

Underneath the steps of Sasha's wagon, Lacertus lay camouflaged like a rock. Stang was not the only one to learn who now possessed the key.

CHAPTER 33

The New Scheme

Lacertus was frantically planning now. *All is not yet lost,* he thought. *I can still get the key safely to Corasar. Someone will have to kill the pretty gypsy girl and then the key can be taken by anyone.* Lacertus knew it would be a difficult task, but not impossible. The problem he faced was that she was so kind and attractive. People don't mind killing nasty and ugly things, but they tended to find a moral compass when their victim was loving and beautiful. He would have to find someone with absolutely no conscience to do the job.

At first, he thought perhaps Stang was a good candidate. He had no qualms about taking the lives of others in the past. But then he realized Stang felt strong, fatherly affection toward the girl, and he thought it was his job to protect her. Stang could be vicious, but he only killed when he thought he had a logical and moral reason for doing so. *No, Stang will not work,* Lacertus thought. *He's too enamored with her, too moral, too intelligent.*

So he realized he needed to find someone who was stupid and completely selfish. Someone who really didn't know the girl, or better yet, someone whose prejudicial way of thinking caused them to look down on her and despise her. *Yes, someone who thinks she is worthless,* he thought. *That is the type of person who could take her life.* Then Arboron came to his mind. Who better to do the job than the one they had picked to bring the key back to Corasar? But then Lacertus remembered how hard it had been to get Arboron out of bed that morning. *He is selfish and despises the girl, but he is also so lazy and lethargic. He is not aggressive enough to kill an innocent victim who has never wronged him.* The lizard did not think he could motivate Arboron to take the girl's life. He needed someone else to do the job. Someone who thought like Arboron and was just as selfish, but who was also pugnacious with a vicious streak. Then it came to him. Arboron's wife, Histrionicah, was the perfect candidate. All he had to do was get her to Sugstal, and the rest would be easy.

* * * * *

Histrionicah walked out of the windship yard in Sugstal, holding her pet lap-frog, Lilypad, followed by two servants hauling a vast amount of her luggage. A little voice in her head had told her she needed to come to Sugstal as quickly as possible. She was angry with her husband, but she was trying to think positively, just like the preacher Telecon taught her. *Maybe Arboron had to get on the windship because they refused to give him a refund,* she thought. *It would be a shame to lose all the money we paid for the fares.*

As she turned to go down High Street toward the *Wayside Inn,* she saw her husband standing next to a distinguished-looking young woman dressed all in orange. They were smiling at each other and engaged in a very animated conversation. Then the woman extended her gloved hand toward Arboron, and he took it in his hand and bent down to kiss it. As she walked away, Arboron stood there with his hat in his hand, admiring her and looking like he was smitten with the girl. Histrionicah walked up behind her husband and punched him in the arm. Startled, he turned around wondering what sort of trouble he was in now. She folded her stubby arms across her chest and scowled at him.

"Histrionicah, darling! What a surprise!" He really was surprised. He never expected for her to show up here.

"Who is she, Arboron? What are you up to?" she demanded.

"Who are you talking about?" He tried to feign innocence, but it was not working. His face was bright red and so were his eyes.

"That orange hussy you were just talking to! Who is she?"

"Oh her! She's no hussy, dear. She is the Princess Gwynneth of the house of Payton; a woman of noble standing and great wealth. She has given me some very sound guidance for finding my forest."

"You looked like you were getting quite chummy with her!"

"No-ooo. Purely business, my dear, purely business," he lied, shaking his head.

They both stood there looking at each other for an awkward moment, and then she said, "Well, where is it?"

"Where is what?"

"The stinking forest!"

"North! To the north of the village. By an orphanage." He continued to stand there wondering what to do next. He was really lost without his inner voice telling him what to do, and he had not planned on his wife showing up.

"Well, don't just stand there! Show it to me!"

"Yes, dear," he mumbled as they started walking toward the North Gate. The two servants started following them with all of her luggage.

"Go to the inn and wait for us there!" Histrionicah commanded the servants. They slowly turned around and walked toward the *Wayside Inn* with all of the trunks and bags.

"This had better be good!" she said to Arboron as she strutted through the gate. "I'll be very upset if I came all this way just to see you fawning over some young floozy!"

"Remember dear, think positively! Think good thoughts!" he reminded her.

"I'll give you good thoughts! So many good thoughts you'll wish you'd never met that tramp!" She hit him hard again in the chest.

"Yes, dear. Yes, you certainly will."

CHAPTER 34

The Rejected Offer

Not far from the North Gate, Arboron and Histrionicah came to a wooden archway. A sign hung across the top held by two iron hinges. The top line read, *Sugstal Orphanage and School for Children* in large letters. The bottom line read, *Let the little children come unto me* in smaller, italicized letters. As they walked through the gate, they were amazed by the giant redwoods that stood on both sides of the path. The broad trees towered high over their heads for as far as they could see.

"This forest is marvelous!" Arboron exclaimed. "I've never seen anything like it, and it's mine! All mine!"

"Yes, dear," Histrionicah sneered, admiring all of the rings on her fingers. "I'm sure we will make a killing when we get rid of all this wood!"

They walked a bit further down the path, until they came to a large, wooden building that blended perfectly into its setting. It looked like it had been built out of the redwoods surrounding it. They walked up the front steps and went inside. After walking down a long hall, they entered a waiting room where they talked to a middle-aged woman who appeared to be a secretary. They explained why they were there, and the secretary invited them to have a seat. She told them the headmistress would see them in a moment.

Lady Elaine was rushing back to her office with a high stack of books in her arms and a thousand different administrative tasks competing in her mind, so she did not even notice the round, green woman and froggy-looking man sitting in the waiting room.

When she dropped the books on her desk, her secretary handed her several papers and said, "There's someone waiting to see you. They say it's important. Something about selling the orphanage?"

"What? Who said that we are for sale?" she said with a look of consternation. She quickly walked back out into the waiting room to find out what this was all about.

"Hello, I am Lady Elaine. I am the headmistress here. How can I help you?" she said to the green couple sitting on the sofa.

"I am Sir Arboron, chairman of the Western Forestry Guild, and this is my wife, Histrionicah," he said standing up and holding out his hand toward his wife. "I have a business proposal for you that I believe you will find very profitable."

"I'm sorry! I am not a businesswoman. I run a school and an orphanage."

"Well, you still need money to run this place, don't you?" Arboron asked.

"Yes, but we depend on donations and the generosity of others."

Histrionicah sneered and shook her head at Lady Elaine as she spoke. The teacher in Lady Elaine could not allow such a childish response go by unchallenged, so turning to Histrionicah she said, "Do you believe it is wrong to ask people to support a work that helps those in need?"

"I believe that if the poor were not so lazy and negative, they could be just as happy as the rest of us," Histrionicah said arrogantly, "but they're too busy mooching off those of us who are positive, wealthy, and successful! They make me sick!"

"And I believe that a helpless, little child who lost her parents in a horrible accident deserves to be loved and protected! And if that means that you have to give up just one of your meaningless parties to feed her, so be it!" Lady Elaine's sense of moral justice had been challenged and she was filled with righteous anger. She knew she was called to love everyone, but she found it really hard to even like these two. The sooner she could get them out of the building, the better.

"Now, now! I see we have a difference of opinion here," Arboron said soothingly. "But we did not come here to discuss the plight of the lower classes. I would like to buy your property from you. I will pay you very handsomely."

"Sorry, it is *not* for sale!" Lady Elaine declared holding up one hand.

"Not even for one million kroner?" Arboron offered.

"No, thank you!"

"How about one and a half million."

"I already told you, the orphanage is *not* for sale."

"Okay, two million! You could take that money and put up a better building anywhere you choose."

"We are very happy here. We will never sell the orphanage."

"You drive a hard bargain. I'll go to two and a half million kroner, but that is my final offer."

"Please leave, we are not interested in your offer!"

"What would it take for you to move out of here and go somewhere else?" Arboron asked. He really thought everyone had their price, because to him it was only about the money. He did not understand people like Lady Elaine. She lived and worked in Sugstal because she loved its natural beauty, and she truly loved the children under her care and the people of the village who supported her work.

"The building would have to be *destroyed* before we moved out of here. We are *not* selling. Please see yourselves out. I have to get back to my work!" She turned and went back into her office, hoping they would leave quickly.

As Arboron and Histrionicah left the building, he said, "I really thought she would jump at my offer of two and a half million. She could build five orphanages with that and still make a huge profit. The woman's a fool!"

"Yes, she is. Did you hear her rant and rave about how we should sacrifice our hard-earned money to feed her horrible little urchins?" Histrionicah sneered.

"She just doesn't get it! She has no idea of how to run a successful business!"

"No, but she did tell us how we can get her property for almost nothing!" Histrionicah was already developing a wicked scheme in her head.

"What do you mean?" he asked.

"She told us, 'The building would have to be *destroyed*.' You want the forest not the building. The building isn't really worth much any way. It would be very *unfortunate* if something happened to make it *uninhabitable*." A wicked sneer appeared on Histrionicah's pale chubby face.

Arboron thought about it for a moment and said, "No, we can't do that. It wouldn't be right."

"But you deserve it, Snookums. You've worked so *hard* for it!" she said coddling him.

"I was meant to own that forest. The trees are so magnificent! I would be really depressed if I didn't get it," he whined.

"Yes, and *that* would not be right. We can't let them treat you so *badly*. Just leave it up to me. I'll take care of it," she whispered as she patted his arm.

A gecko hung on to the back of her hat. It had whispered the whole diabolical plan in her ear. When they got to the North Gate, it jumped down to meet with Lacertus and Nefario by the side of the road. "It's done!" it reported.

"Good!" the lizard said. "Now for the hard part."

CHAPTER 35

The Wicked Deed

On the next Day of Resting, as usual, Sasha put on her embroidered, white dress, her best boots, and her sword over her shoulder, and she headed toward the prayerhouse. As she walked through the woods, she felt like someone was following her. She turned around and saw Stang walking up behind her.

"Going to pray again, lass?" he said.

"Of course!" she said as she turned around and starting walking toward the village again.

"Mind if I come with you?" he asked stepping up beside her.

She felt like saying that she did mind, because she still did not trust Stang. But all that she had been taught told her that it would be wrong to turn someone away from the prayerhouse, so she said nothing and just kept walking.

It felt strange walking through the village with Stang by her side. All the men scowled at him. The women who would usually give her cheerful greetings gave looks of consternation instead. One woman even whispered, "Are you okay?" to her behind Stang's back. The little children were frightened by this large, intimidating man in black, and they hid behind their mothers' skirts. When they got to the prayerhouse, Sasha felt relieved, because Stang stood in the back as she sat down in her usual seat toward the front.

Ebesian and his students sat up on the right side of the balcony, along with Ansen, Ben and Nathan. Most of the orphans sat toward the back, in the middle of the balcony. Lady Elaine was taking a head count and she noticed seven children and Tasca were missing.

"Please go out and find the children from the third-floor dorm room," she said to her assistant. "They seemed to have lost their way here." The young assistant shook her head and retraced her steps back toward the orphanage.

As the people were about to begin praying, Lady Elaine's assistant came running down the main aisle of the prayerhouse in a panic. She shouted, "Fire! Fire! The orphanage is on fire! I think some of the children and Tasca are still inside!"

Everyone immediately stood up and someone began to frantically ring the bell in the tower. The whole congregation left the building and ran toward the orphanage with any buckets they could find. Soon, lines of villagers were passing pails full of water from the well in the courtyard toward where the building was burning.

From a window on the third floor, some of the children were crying for help. One of them was Litfim. Ben said to Nathan, "We have to do something. Is there a ladder somewhere?" As they went to search for a ladder, Ben noticed a tall woodsman standing nearby. He ran straight over to him.

"I know who you are!" Ben said to the woodsman. "You're the engven who has been protecting Litfim. I remember meeting you when I was just a boy. You saved my life that day. Please save Tasca and Litfim now!"

Anskar said, "Litfim will not only survive today, but he and the boys who are rescued now will one day come to your aid when all hope is gone. But for the Highest One's plan to be accomplished you must stay close to the gypsy girl named Sasha. Is that clear?"

"Yes! I understand."

"Do not hesitate to act, Bensareon! The key must not fall into the hands of the enemy!" Anskar said as he patted Ben on the back and ran toward the fire.

"The key?" Ben whispered with astonishment. "What do I have to do with the key?" Then he ran off to find Sasha.

Sasha was standing near the burning building wondering what she could do to help. She had been given the key for a reason, but what could she do with it to help the children inside? The woodsman had not given her any instructions, so she decided to pray.

* * * * *

Histrionicah gleefully watched the results of her wicked deed in the woods near the fire. She wanted to make sure there was nothing left of the building when it was all over. Lacertus, Nefario and the gecko were also there, feverishly working on her demented mind.

"Look!" the gecko whispered in her ear. "There's that girl my husband was with the other day!" They knew Histrionicah was very nearsighted from her poor diet. The orange flames of the fire reflected off Sasha's white dress as she stood in the shadows of the tall redwoods near the building. "She's in the same orange dress!" it hissed. The nekron were hoping she was so filled with hatred she would fall for the ruse.

"Can it be her?" Histrionicah said out loud.

"Yes, that's the same one!" Nefario prompted her.

"I can't stand that hussy!" Histrionicah sneered.

"Wouldn't it be convenient if she happened to go missing in the fire?" Nefario said.

"Yes, it would!" she said with a fiendish grin. "Very convenient!"

CHAPTER 36

The Daring Rescue

Ben saw Sasha praying with a small group of people near the building, so he ran over to her. As he approached her, a large gypsy dressed in black blocked his path.

"I'm here to talk to Sasha," Ben said trying to get around the big gypsy.

"And I'm here to *protect* her," Stang said.

"So am I!" Ben retorted.

"You don't look like much of a bodyguard."

"Maybe! But I still have to talk to her. It's very important!"

While Ben and Stang were arguing over her security, Sasha felt led to unsheathe her sword and go into the building. As she held the sword in her hand, words from the Lore flooded over her mind: "Whatever you did for one of my brothers or sisters, no matter how unimportant they seemed to be, you did for me."[4]

As she came up to the burning building, the flames were blocking all entrances, and out of fear she was tempted to give up trying to get inside. "Perfect love drives out all fear!"[5] the Lore reminded her. She stepped forward holding the sword in front of her, and a bright, violet light shone out from the blade. It created a violet bubble of protection around her. As she moved toward the flames, they parted in front of her and danced around the bubble without touch-

---

4   Matthew 25:40.
5   1 John 4:18.

ing her. She felt exhilarated by the experience and shouted for joy. As she moved through the hallway, violet flowers carpeted the floor. "Ehadre-els!" she exclaimed as she remembered their name. "The flowers of the Eternal City!" Although she was tempted to linger there, she remembered she did not have much time to save the children, so she ran up the nearest staircase with her sword protecting her the whole way.

Outside, Ben and Stang stopped arguing long enough to notice that Sasha was gone. When they began looking around for her, Ben spotted her and said, "Over there! She's going into the building!"

They both ran toward the doorway as she stepped into the burning building. Stang started to go inside, but a fireball exploded out of the doorway just as he was entering. He fell back onto the ground with all the hair singed off his face. Stang shouted a curse at the flames, and kicked up the dirt toward the doorway. Then he turned toward Ben and shouted, "If any harm comes to her, I am holding you responsible!"

Ben and Stang frantically ran around the building looking for another way in, but the flames were erupting out of every door and window on the lower level.

Sasha found seven boys and Tasca up in the third-floor dorm room. The ceiling was on fire, the back wall was burning, and the floor looked like it was about give way. "Come, quickly!" Sasha commanded them. They all ran toward her but they could not all fit within the bubble. Sasha looked at Tasca with dismay and shouted, "I'll have to take some of you now and come back for the rest!"

"There's no time for a second trip!" Tasca shouted. "Allow me to help!" She unsheathed her sword and touched Sasha's sword with it. It also glowed bright violet, and the bubble extended around them all.

"I wish someone would tell me all that this thing can do!" Sasha said to Tasca. Then she said to the children, "Follow the violet flowers on the floor and you'll all be safe!"

As they walked down the first stairway together she found it hard to move because all of the boys clung to her. "You have to give me room to walk," she said. "Don't crowd me. You'll all be okay. Just give me a little more room."

It took less time to move down the second stairway. The boys became more confident about moving away from her as they saw how the bubble still extended to protect them. But when they got down to the first floor they all ran back to her and screamed when the floor above them gave way. Debris came crashing down all around them and a large beam now rested across the top of the bubble. Sasha moved forward slightly and then she stopped when she realized everything might cave in on them if she went any further.

Tasca walked around Sasha and moved toward the door. The bubble now extended in front of the group all the way to the doorway. "Run through the door!" she commanded the boys. When they all hesitated she shouted, "Go!" and they all ran out of the building screaming.

"The boys are all safe! Let's go!" Tasca shouted to Sasha.

"I'm right behind you!" Sasha shouted back.

Just as Tasca ran through the doorway, Histrionicah stepped into the hallway behind Sasha holding a dagger. "So you want to take Arboron away from me, you little tramp!" she sneered. She did not see the sword or the violet bubble holding up what was left of the building.

Sasha turned half way around and said, "What are you talking about? I don't know anyone named Arboron!"

"Don't lie to me. I saw you with him."

"I don't know who you're talking about! Lady, we need to get out of here!"

In a fit of rage, Histrionicah ran toward Sasha and slashed at her with the dagger. Sasha tried to block the blow. The dagger sliced her arm and she dropped her sword. The violet bubble disappeared and the building came crashing down all around them. Burning boards fell on top of Sasha and knocked her off her feet, not far from the doorway. Histrionicah was killed instantly as the large beam came straight down on her head.

Ben and Stang ran into the building to get Sasha out. Ben threw the boards off her, and Stang lifted her up and carried her limp body outside. Ben found her sword and took it with him. "Healer! Healer!" he shouted to the crowd that had gathered outside.

Gransen ran forward with a medical bag in his hand. He knelt down by Sasha and felt for a pulse. Her heart had stopped and she was not breathing. He put his mouth on hers and breathed air into her lungs. Then he checked for a pulse again. He repeated this process many times. Then he said, "I'm sorry, she's gone! There's nothing more I can do."

For the first time in his life, Stang openly expressed compassion for another person. He held Sasha's head close to his and wept on her neck. Everyone else in the village wept as well.

Just at that moment, Ben saw a violet flash out of the corner of his eye. He had left Sasha's sword on the ground about twelve feet away. As the life went out of Sasha's body, her sword disappeared and the violet key appeared in its place.

"What an interesting treasure!" Arboron said as he bent over to pick up the key. As he touched it, the key began to twist and turn yellow green. In the woods nearby, Lacertus prompted his victim. The plan was coming together perfectly.

Ben remembered Anskar's warning not to hesitate but to take action. He grabbed hold of the hilt of his sword, and in one fluid motion he unsheathed it and threw it toward the key on the ground. It hit the key, glanced off the ground, and flew back around into his hand. All that Arboron saw was a sudden flash of light, and the strange object disappeared just before he could grab hold of it.

Off in the woods nearby, Lacertus and Nefario were shouting curses and beating the ground with the black chains attached to their bodies. Ben quickly put his sword away. Most of the people present did not even see what had happened because they were mourning so deeply for Sasha.

CHAPTER 37

The Signed Contract

Lady Elaine and a crowd of people watched as the last part of the orphanage collapsed in flames. In tears, she turned and said to her assistants, "Pray that we will be able to rebuild someday," and she started walking back toward the village all alone. Arboron had been standing near the orphanage gate waiting to talk to her. He did not know where his wife was, but he thought their plan was coming together perfectly.

"Lady Elaine," he said when he saw her. "I'm so sorry to see what has happened."

She stopped and said, "Losing the orphanage is nothing compared to that young girl losing her life."

"What a tragedy," he said shaking his head with mock compassion. "But perhaps some good could still come out of all this."

"What do you mean?" she asked.

"Well, I am still willing to buy the orphanage from you. Let's say five hundred thousand kroner?"

"The other day you said you would pay us five times as much."

"Yes, but there is not much left of the building now, so I think five hundred is the best I can do."

"Thank you, Mr. Arboron. I accept your offer." She shook his hand. "I will ask my attorney to draw up the papers and we can sign them tomorrow morning at his office. It's located in the northern part of the village. Look for the offices of Lawson and Lawson."

"I'll see you there tomorrow!" he said smiling. The plan had worked perfectly. He had to find Histrionicah and tell her the good news.

As Lady Elaine walked away, she praised the Highest One. With that money, they would be able to build an even better and larger building. Who thought that someone like Arboron would be so generous? Maybe she had misjudged him.

*   *   *   *   *

The next morning, Arboron did something very unusual—he got up before eight o'clock in the morning. He was very excited about acquiring his new forest. He did not know where Histrionicah was, but he assumed that she was in her room at the inn. She had told him that since she was still angry about seeing him with "that hussy" she was not going to sleep in the same bed with him. He had gladly agreed to pay for another room so that he did not have to listen to her constant whining and nagging.

Arboron got dressed and he put the strap of his leather satchel over his shoulder. It had five hundred thousand kroner in it. He knew from his vast business experience that real estate transactions were always conducted in cash. He left the inn and walked toward the northern end of the village. The offices of Lawson and Lawson were easy to find. A large sign marked the wood and stucco building. He went inside and a friendly secretary invited him to take a seat inside of one of their tidy offices. "Mr. Lawson will be with you shortly," she said.

Just a few moments later, Lawson entered the room, followed by a smiling Lady Elaine and a large man in a dark suit. Lawson sat down behind the desk, and Lady Elaine sat across from him in a padded chair next to Arboron. The large man appeared to be security personnel, since he remained standing next to the door with his hands together in front of him.

Lawson was a short, older man. He was very fit for his age, and he always wore a suit and tie. His clothes were perfectly pressed, and his hair and beard were perfectly trimmed. Lawson was always all business, and he never engaged in small talk.

"Lady Elaine asked me to draw up a contract to transfer ownership of the orphanage over to you, Mr. Arboron. Here it is. Please read it, and if it is to your liking, please sign it. There are also two other copies to sign. One for Lady Elaine and one for my records."

Arboron quickly glanced over the contract. The names of the parties were right and so was the amount he was to pay. The rest of the contract seemed to be the usual legal mumbo jumbo, assigning to him all the rights and responsibilities of the property and protecting the seller from possible lawsuits. He grabbed a pen and said, "It looks good to me," and he signed it and the other copies. Lady Elaine also signed all the contracts. She had read it over carefully and thoroughly discussed it with Lawson earlier that morning.

Arboron handed the satchel over to Lawson, and Lawson signaled to the man at the door to come over and count the money inside the bag. He stacked it neatly on the desk as he counted out five hundred thousand kroner. "It's all here, sir," said the large man.

"Thank you, Lars," Lawson said. "Please place it in Lady Elaine's bag." Lars placed all the money in the bag Lady Elaine had with her, and then he went back to stand by the door.

Lawson stood up and shook Lady Elaine's hand. She was smiling brightly. Arboron also stood up as well. "Thank you, Mr. Arboron, for your generosity," she said as she shook his hand as well.

"Oh, the pleasure is all mine," Arboron said with a big grin.

As Arboron shook Lawson's hand, Lady Elaine left the room with a copy of the contract and the five hundred thousand kroner. "It was a pleasure doing business with you as well, Mr. Lawson," he said as he turned to leave with the contract in his hand.

"Thank you. Please be sure to remove all of the debris from my land by the end of the month," Lawson said.

Arboron turned back toward Lawson and said, "What are you talking about?"

"You now own the burnt-out building that is on my property. The contract clearly states that it is your responsibility to remove it," Lawson said calmly.

"But the land is now *mine*!" Arboron said in disbelief.

"Oh no, sir. You purchased the building, not the land it sits on. The land belongs to me. My family has owned the wood for generations. I leased it to the orphanage for one krone a year for the last twenty years."

"But I thought I was buying the *forest*, not just the *building*!" he said getting angry now.

Lawson laughed at him and said, "Sir, you call yourself a businessman! Any boy just out of business school knows you read a contract before you sign it!"

"You swindled me, you crook!" Arboron threatened waving his fist in the air. Lars now came over and stood very close to his boss.

"I did not attempt to defraud you in any way, sir, and I gave you ample opportunity to read the contract. You willingly gave Lady Elaine the money without any coercion!"

"I am going to take you to court! I'll sue you for every penny you've got!" Arboron ranted.

"Go ahead! The case will be heard here at the local courthouse in Sugstal, and I happen to know the only judge in the village very well. He is my brother and co-owner of Lawson's Wood!"

"But, but, but . . . I got absolutely nothing for my money!" Arboron stammered.

"You received the blessing of knowing that you helped the orphanage get back on their feet after a terrible accident. They will now be able to construct that new building they've always wanted and even have money to spare!"

Arboron was at a loss for words and he just stood there with his mouth hanging open in shock. So Lawson said, "Good day to you, sir! Lars will accompany you out!"

Lars stepped between Lawson and Arboron. When Arboron did not move immediately, Lars grabbed the back of his collar and pushed him toward the door. He shoved him through the waiting room and out the front entrance. Arboron tumbled down the stairs and landed in the mud.

Arboron began to cry. He slowly stood up and wandered toward the orphanage. Although he had made billions of kroner over the years, he had spent every last one, and borrowed billions more. He was deeply in debt, and it was impossible for him to pay back his creditors. He was counting on buying the orphanage's forest to get himself out of the financial nightmare he was in. He was ruined—completely bankrupt! He did not know how to tell his wife. When she found out, she would definitely kill him. He could not bear the thought of facing her. He hated Histrionicah, and he hated his life. So he took what he assumed was the easiest way out of his troubles. He jumped off the cliff close to the lighthouse, and plunged to his death at the bottom of the fjord.

The next thing Arboron knew was that he was standing in a vast area that was extremely cold and dark. There was nothing to be seen for miles in every direction, except for a bright, white light in the distance and a column of pitch-black smoke rising up from the ground to the left of it. After he had walked for a while toward the light, he heard someone shouting his name. He turned, and to his shock and dismay, it was Histrionicah.

"Where have you been, Arboron? I've been calling for you for hours!" she whined.

When he came close to where she was standing, he saw that her head had been smashed in and it was horribly mutilated. It looked like an egg that had been cracked open for breakfast after the top had been taken off with a spoon.

"Where are we?" he asked looking away from her horrible deformity.

"I don't know, but I hate this stinking place! I demand you find someone to get us out of here immediately!" she insisted.

"But I don't even know where 'here' is!" he said staring out into the darkness.

"Well, I suggest you figure it out before I start to get really angry!" she shouted.

"And what are you going to do then, Histrionicah? Throw another temper tantrum?" he shouted back.

"I can make life miserable for you, darling! And don't think that I won't do it! I killed your little hussy. Don't think I won't kill you!"

Arboron had had enough. He flew into a rage and started punching her with his fists. When he punched at her chest his hand went right through her body, as if nothing was there. Startled, he stopped what he was doing and fell backwards on to the ground in shock and disbelief.

Histrionicah pulled open her blouse to reveal a large hole that went straight through her chest. She screamed in horror and started wildly shaking her hands back and forth in front of what was left of her body. She finally realized that she had no heart, and it would have scared her to death if she was not already dead! Shrieking with terror, she ran off toward the white light in the distance and her doom.

CHAPTER 38

The Humble Guardian

Ben and Ebesian stood by the simple stone that marked Sasha's grave. The whole village had come to the funeral service. It had lasted for hours, since so many people wanted to tell stories of Sasha's kindness and generosity. Now everyone had gone back to their homes to try to somehow continue their lives without her.

On the walk back into the village, Ben asked the loremaster, "Why are your students giving me the cold shoulder?"

"They're upset because they thought that one of them would be chosen to relight the beacon," Ebesian said quietly. "They have been studying and training for this for years. Large expectations are hard to relinquish."

"I had no other option, professor. It's not like I was looking for this!" Ben said. "The engven told me what to do, and when the time came, I just did what had to be done. I couldn't let the key fall into the hands of the enemy."

"No, you did the right thing. Don't worry about the students. They'll get over their jealousy. You have been chosen, and they just have to accept that."

"Perhaps I'll die like Sasha, and then one of your students can *have* the key," Ben said wishing that his sword had never melded with it.

"No, I don't believe that is your destiny. Everything happens for a reason. There is no such thing as coincidence only providence, and Providence has chosen *you*."

"Well, then a *failure* has just been chosen to bear the Murastan!"

"Is that what you think you are, a *failure?*" Ebesian challenged.

"Yes, and the High Council agrees! They sent me back to Sugstal after I lost every man in my unit in the Darklands. I failed! Miserably!"

"So now you're a useless failure! Is that what you are telling me?" the loremaster said looking him straight in the eye.

Ben did not respond. He knew that was not true. Instead, he sighed, shook his head slightly, and looked down at the ground.

"Good! We wouldn't want a guardian of one of the seven keys to be conceited. I'm glad to hear it's *not* going to go to your head!" Ebesian declared, as he patted Ben on the forehead. "Remember, the Highest One uses those who are humble, so praise him for knocking you down a few pegs!"

As Ebesian walked away, Ben realized that he was about to face a huge challenge, and the loremaster was not about to coddle him.

CHAPTER 39

The Violet Light

The next morning, Ben, Jon, Tasca, and Traven walked down the path toward Viridan's dilapidated mansion with their swords in their hands. They knew that somewhere in this area, the ancient beacon once stood, and now they had to find it. The four of them were to search the house. Landron and Gransen were assigned the task of searching the woods to the east of the mansion, between the mansion and the fjord. They were already walking along a path that ran along the edge of the cliff. Ebesian and Mandar waited for the students on the South Road.

"According to Ebesian's map, the tower stood over toward the northeastern corner of the house," Traven said looking down at the parchment in his hand. "Of course, the house was built later, so it might be difficult to find the beacon's foundation under all the later construction."

When they came to the front steps of the mansion, Jon said, "We'll cover more ground if we separate. Tasca and I will search the first floor. You two can cover the upper levels." Jon nodded his head toward Tasca, and he walked around the chandelier that had smashed to the floor and on through the doors to the great hall. Tasca looked back at Ben and Traven, and then she followed Jon into the darkness beyond the large double doors.

Traven whispered what Ben was thinking, "Why does *he* always get to be with Tasca?" Ben shrugged his shoulders. "I don't think we're going to find the tower up there," Traven said pointing to the double staircases. "We should be looking around outside, to see if we can find any ancient foundation stones."

"Okay. You look around outside," Ben replied. "I'll take the upstairs." Traven ran out the front doors and down the steps, as Ben began to climb the right staircase.

When Ben got to the top of the stairs, he thought he saw a dark shape slither across the far end of the long hallway. He drew his sword, and it began to glow with a violet light. A lizard hissed and shielded its eyes with its front paw when the light revealed its location in the shadows. It quickly scurried into one of the many rooms at the end of the hallway and slammed the door shut behind it.

"Maybe this is the right direction after all," Ben whispered to himself, as he cautiously walked down the hallway toward where the lizard was hiding. He slowly turned the doorknob and then pushed the door open, holding his sword out in front of him. When he looked inside the room he saw that it was filled with amazing treasures. The floor was covered with gold and silver coins two or three feet deep. Golden candle sticks, silver chests and all kinds of jewelry shone in mahogany cases against all of the walls. It was a treasure fit for a king.

"It is all yours, all yours," croaked five frogs in unison from the far side of the room, but Ben did not see them. Two frogs croaked, "Gree-dee, Gree-dee." A green gas flooded the room, and yellow-green dust clouds emanated from the frogs. The gleam of the treasure all around him caused him to squint because it hurt his eyes. The room began to spin and Ben felt dizzy. "All yours! All yours!" the frogs chanted. As Ben fell to his knees and let go of his sword, he grabbed fists full of gold and silver coins in both hands.

"This is mine?" he asked out loud. He began to get excited at the thought that he would never have to worry about money again. He would be able to buy anything he wanted.

"Yes, it's all yours! It's all yours!" the frogs repeated. One frog croaked, "Gree-dee, Gree-dee." Ben threw the coins up in the air, and then he clutched a pile of coins to his chest.

A lizard crawled up on top of a nearby trophy case. It was Lacertus. With a sinister smile, he hissed, "We've been waiting for you, Murastan! Welcome home!"

Ben looked down, and he saw his sword faintly glowing among the piles of money. His head began to clear slightly, and his eyes were able to focus on the blade. He dropped the coins and took hold of the hilt of the sword. He stood up and held it straight out in front of him. He came to his senses as a verse from the Lore filled his mind.

"'Great gain is godliness with contentment!'"[6] Ben shouted. The sword burst into a brilliant, violet light. All the treasure in the room disintegrated into a pile of yellow-green dust. It had all been an illusion created by the frogs, and now Ben saw that nothing was really there except broken, wooden cases and cobwebs.

"*No!*" shouted Lacertus. "Curses on you! Curses from the depths of the Abyss!"

Ben threw his sword in a perfect arc toward the lizard. Lacertus darted out of the path of the blade, but it slashed off a third of his tail. He scurried off the top of the trophy case into the shadows. Lacertus was bleeding badly. The pain from his injury and the loss of blood were making him dizzy. He decided to slip out a window and nurse his wound in the courtyard down below. The frogs would have to defend the tower without him. He scurried down into a storm drain in the courtyard and followed the pipe out to the fjord.

The frogs began to frantically hop in different directions. Ben tossed his blade toward the nearest one and it made a little fart noise as it stared at the blade coming right toward its head. It popped into a cloud of black and green ash. Ben took out two more of the frogs with one more toss of his sword. Another frog jumped out of a window. The last frog sat perfectly still. It was Nefario. He decided he could still tempt this Tavonian to give in to greed.

"What do you really want more than anything in all of Varden?" Nefario asked, trying to sound innocent and harmless.

---

[6] 1 Timothy 6:6.

"'What does it profit a man if he gains all of Varden yet he loses his own soul?'"[7] Ben responded quoting the Lore.

"Surely there is something you need. Something that you wish you always had. I can give that to you. All you have to do is desire it and it's yours." Nefario put on his cute, Lilypad face. In the past, it always totally disarmed his victims and put them at ease. They did not believe that something so innocent-looking could harm them.

"Yes, you can give me something," Ben whispered. "Something I've wanted ever since Sasha died." The toad smiled. He was confident that his tempting skills were infallible. "I need to see you and all your kind burning in the flames of the Abyss forever! Praise King Tavon!" Ben shouted, as he threw his sword directly at Nefario. The toad tried to jump out of the path of the blade, but it curved toward him as it blazed with a brilliant, violet light. Nefario felt the sword tear through his chest. The pain was agonizing as the blade ripped through his blackened heart. With a terrifying scream, Nefario exploded into green goo. All that was left of him was a puff of black smoke and the faint smell of the perfume used at The Frogorium.

Ben turned around, looking to make sure there were no more nekron in the room. Traven came running in just at that moment.

"Are you all right?" Traven asked.

"Yes, I had a bit of run in with some toads and a lizard." Ben went over to the window to see if he could see any sign of the frog that leapt out the window.

"This location must be important since they were so eager to defend it." Traven began looking under piles of debris.

"What exactly are we looking for?" Ben asked.

"A keyhole in an ancient stone. The Murastan will be able to open the lock."

Ben and Traven began looking around the room for anything that appeared to be a keyhole. They pushed aside old cabinets and furniture, but they found nothing. Finally, they both sat down on the floor and leaned against a wall.

---

[7] Mark 8:36

"Maybe it's somewhere else," Ben said. "The toads may have been trying to deceive us into thinking this is the spot when it's not."

"No, I don't think so." Traven took Ebesian's map out of his pocket and unfolded it on the floor. Pointing to a spot on the northeastern corner of the map he said, "The map shows that it has to be here as well. If not, it's very close to here."

Ben looked up and he saw a square outline in the center of the ceiling. "We're looking for a tower, right? So we should be looking up!" He jumped to his feet and Traven stood up next to him. "Let's get some of this furniture piled up here so that we can get up there," he said, pointing at the square shape above them.

Once they dragged several cabinets and shelves together in the middle of the room, Traven climbed up and pushed against the center of the ceiling. It easily opened like a trap door, and he cautiously poked his head into the opening.

"All clear! This looks like what we're searching for!" Traven said excitedly. "Come on up!" Then he pushed himself up through the opening. Ben climbed up and joined him on a spiral stairway made of stone that ascended up about two more stories.

Out of the corner of his eye, Ben thought he saw someone standing next to Traven in the darkness. But when he focused his eyes in that direction, the figure seemed to melt away into the stone wall. He hesitated climbing up the stairs for a moment until Traven called to him.

"What's the matter?" Traven said, stepping back down a few of the stairs.

"Did you see anyone? I thought someone was standing right next to you." Ben waved his sword back and forth in the air where he thought he saw the other man.

"There's no one else here! You're just imagining things. Creepy places like this will do that to your head. Let's go!"

As they continued up the staircase, Ben knew it was not just something he imagined, so he mumbled, "I hope he's on our side."

At the top of the staircase, they entered a small, circular room made out of old stone. Large windows ran all around the perimeter of the room, and in the center of the room was a stone pillar, about three feet high. Traven walked around the pillar. Then he knelt down to look at a shape that had been carved into the stone. He stood up and smiled broadly. "This is it! There's a keyhole right here!"

Ben walked around and knelt down to examine the carving in the stone. Sure enough, it looked just like a keyhole, and just the right size for the Murastan. "What do we do now, Lore expert?" he asked.

"You just put the key in the keyhole and turn it," Traven said with smirk on his face.

"Seems too easy," Ben said as he looked down at his sword. The key had attached itself to the side of the blade just under the hilt. He placed his left hand over the key and it disengaged from the sword. He gently inserted the key in the slot and slowly turned it clockwise. The entire room started shaking, and a low-pitched rumbling noise became louder as it began to rise in frequency.

"Run!" Traven shouted, as he bolted toward the stairs.

Ben flew down the stairs after him. They jumped through the trap door and slid down the pile of cabinets. The ceiling was crashing down all around them as they ran toward the hallway. The floor gave way in front of them as they stepped out into the hall. They jumped across the hole and ran toward the foyer staircases. The entire mansion was violently shaking now. A loud, crashing noise came from the other side of the house, as the whole east side of the mansion collapsed. Ben hoped that Tasca and Jon were able to escape before the building came smashing down on top of them.

Ben and Traven flew down the stairs and out of the front doors just as the whole west side of the house exploded. Half way down the path, Ben turned around to look back. An intense violet blast knocked him off his feet as it sent shockwaves across the landscape. The ground shook with a violent earthquake. Then a high-pitched noise grew louder and increased in frequency. It was followed by a flash of intense white light, and a tremendously loud boom that shattered the air around them. The actual structure of the things around them seemed to melt away. The very fabric of the objects around them seemed to be vibrating. They covered their heads and prayed that they were not going to die.

CHAPTER 40

The Dramatic Change

The huge explosion could be felt for miles in every direction. The people in Sugstal thought that the mountain had given way and fallen into the fjord, but there was only minor damage in the village. A few people lost trinkets they had grown overly attached to, but no one lost anything of real value or importance. So when the light from the beacon was seen in Sugstal, the people cheered. Many gathered at the prayerhouse to praise the Highest One, even those who had not been there in years.

Like the people in the village, no one in the gypsy camp lost anything of great worth, except for a woman named Felecia. She used to boast that she had the most expensive wagon in the camp, but during the earthquake, the wheels on one side of her wagon fell off and it flipped over on its side. She wept when she saw that all of her fine china dishes had been smashed to pieces.

When the Violet Light blasted through the gypsy camp, all evidence of the yellow-green dust trail from the key disappeared. Even the green stain on Stang's black gloves vanished. Although no one really noticed, Sasha's empty basket in her wagon was now filled with violet Ehadre-el flowers.

The people across the fjord in Corasar did not do as well. They thought it was the end of the world. And for them, it was. The capital city of Babbelar melted away, as the shops on Purchase Street vanished, and the financial district completely disappeared. Many of the Corasarians became homeless as their houses vaporized before their eyes.

When the earthquake hit Babbelar, the women in the shops began screaming and running from the buildings into the street. Everyone was in a state of total panic. As the Violet Light blasted across the city, anyone holding a lap-frog watched in terror as the creatures exploded in their arms. The frogs dissolved into puffs of black smoke, leaving their owners faces and clothes covered in thick, green, mucus-like goo. Many of those who witnessed the destruction of the frogs shrieked in terror, trying to spit the foul-tasting slime out of their mouths. Others were so frightened they could not move or even make a sound. All they could do was tremble in shock and horror. Some fainted dead away, or even had a heart attack.

After the violet shockwave passed over Babbelar, the illusion created by the greed of thousands of wicked hearts disappeared. Now everyone saw the city for what it really was. The large mansions were really just small, dilapidated shacks. The soaring towers were really just rusted out metal skeletons. The piles of treasure were really just heaps of trash. The fancy clothes were just worthless rags. Babbelar was really just a large garbage dump. It had always been that way, but few people saw it before because their greed and materialism had blinded them to the truth. Now the spell of the enemy had been broken, and everyone saw the city for what it truly was—a huge pile of filthy, stinking rubbish. The people of Babbelar wept when they realized they had just been living in a large landfill all their lives.

When the earthquake began to shake the Renown Tower, Capitalo's staff fled from the tall building, running for their lives. Many people fell down on their knees in the street, and they began begging the Highest One to rescue them. Everyone escaped from the tower except for Capitalo who was too busy making a big business deal to leave. When the tower started shaking, he just ignored it, and he kept on negotiating with a client over the crystal ball in his office. His company had built the tower, and he had confidence that a little tremor could not cause any major damage to such a magnificent building. Besides, he had to close this deal right away. If he waited another day, he would lose millions of kroner. As the Violet Light blasted through the Renown Tower the entire building vanished into thin air along with everything in it, including Capitalo. He had no time to pray or set his affairs in order. The Violet Light instantly shattered his body into millions of tiny particles.

The next thing Capitalo knew was that he was standing in a vast area that was extremely cold and dark. There was nothing to be seen for miles in every direction, except for a bright, white light in the distance and a column of pitch-black smoke rising up from the ground just to the left of it. He slowly stumbled toward the light and his doom. His heart was filled with terror when he stood before the Judge, and every one of his secret schemes were revealed by the One who knows everything.

The large amphitheater where Telecon spoke was filled to capacity when the earthquake hit the city. The huge dome over the building came crashing down on the crowds inside and many people died, including Telecon himself. Those who lost their lives also found themselves standing in that vast, cold, dark space near the Abyss and the Great White Throne. At first, they were all very confused about where they were, but soon people began to figure out that they had died and that judgement now awaited them.

Telecon stumbled around all alone in the darkness for a long time. It was days before he finally realized he needed to walk toward the white light very far off in the distance. When he finally got close to the Great White Throne, people in the crowd recognized him, but he did not receive the welcome he expected. Those who saw Telecon were seething with hatred toward him. They had come to realize that they were all facing endless misery, because they had believed Telecon's lies.

One man started shouting, "Throw Telecon into the Abyss! Let's not wait for the Judge to decide his fate!" It was Arboron, who was still waiting for his own case to be heard.

The members of the angry mob agreed, and they started chanting, "Throw him into the Abyss! Throw him into the Abyss!"

"Think positively!" Telecon pleaded, with terror in his eyes. "Good fortune is coming if you only believe!"

No one listened to him. Instead they threw things at him, they started beating him with their fists, and they kept shouting, "Throw him into the Abyss!"

Telecon tried to beg for mercy, but the mob was not in a very positive or charitable mood. So they lifted him up on their shoulders and carried him over to the brink of the Abyss. Then, without a moment's hesitation, they tossed him head first into the endless, burning darkness.

* * * *

Where Viridan's mansion once stood there was now a tall stone tower at the northeastern corner of a square fortress. The beacon and the stone walls appeared to be ancient, yet at the same time they appeared to be brand new. In the middle of the fortress was a courtyard with a beautiful garden, filled with all kinds of fruit trees. A bright, violet light shone from the tower. It had the power to change everything it illuminated, so that the entire area glimmered with a new-found sense of beauty and value. Anyone who saw the light was overwhelmed with a sense of peace and contentment.

Ben noticed that the Murastan had reattached itself to his blade, and it shone with a new, brilliant, violet light. It reminded him of Sasha, and he wished that she could have seen the amazing results of her sacrifice.

Back on the South Road, Ebesian and Mandar wept with their arms around each other's shoulders. They both felt fifty years younger. One of the beacons had finally been restored after years and years of hard work and sacrifice. Mandar had thought he would never live to see this day. Ebesian scolded himself for ever doubting it would happen.

As they walked back to the inn, Ebesian lamented to his friend, "There are six more keys to go! The quest is only going to become much harder from here on out!"

"I knew it! I knew it! You did it again!" Mandar shouted. "Do you always have to throw a wet blanket on a celebration? You should be thrilled that we relit one of the seven beacons! We're talking about an event of historic proportions! Would it really kill you to be excited about that?"

"Excitement is highly overrated. Besides, we're far from finished, and I'm not getting any younger!" Ebesian said as he remembered the puzzle box in his pocket. A frustrated Mandar just shook his head at his old friend.

Meanwhile, Ben and Traven went looking for Jon and Tasca, and they found them in the fortress garden, eating fruit off the trees.

"You could have warned us before you did that, Bensareon!" Jon chided with a smile as he gave Ben a gentle shove.

"Yes, you almost killed us!" Tasca said, punching Ben's arm with one hand and eating a pear with the other.

"I thought Traven knew how the thing worked!" Ben retorted.

"Don't blame me! It's not like I go around relighting beacons every day!" Traven said defensively.

"Here, try this. It's delicious!" Jon said, as he tossed a peach to Ben.

Ben bit into the peach and the juice ran down his chin. It was the sweetest, most luscious thing he had ever eaten. He had never even seen a peach before that day. Now he was wondering if he could live in the garden and eat peaches every day.

All four of them sampled all of the fruit in the garden. There were peaches, strawberries, apples, pears, bananas, cherries, grapes and mangos. There were also other kinds of fruit they could not even identify. After eating their fill, they sat on the warm grass in the center of the courtyard looking up at the soaring tower. A warm, violet light bathed the entire area. It changed everything it touched, so that everything seemed to be richer and more meaningful. It made them feel at peace and filled them with a sense of wonder and contentment. At that moment, they did not have a care in the world.

"It's beautiful!" Tasca said with a dreamy look in her eye. "So peaceful. So right somehow."

"Yeah, it really is!" Ben agreed. "You know, this would be a great location for the new orphanage."

"What a great idea!" Tasca shouted. "We'll have to talk to Lady Elaine when we get back to the village."

They all stood up and waited there a moment longer, just basking in the light. Then Jon shouted, "We did it!" All four of them drew their swords and tossed them high in the air as they thanked the Highest One for their success. They hugged and congratulated each other, and then they headed down the road back toward Sugstal, with full bellies and broad smiles on their faces.

When Ben hugged Tasca, it was more warmhearted than the hugs she received from Jon and Traven. It was a caring, loving embrace. She realized he cared deeply for her. She had not really noticed it before, but now she did. She decided she needed to learn more about the young windship captain who thought of sharing the fruit of paradise with orphans instead of keeping it for himself.

When Ben and Tasca returned to the village, they immediately went to talk to Lady Elaine about their idea. From Lawson, they discovered Viridan had no family and no heirs. He also left no will, because he thought he would never die. Therefore, the land where his mansion once stood became the property of the village of Sugstal. When the village council met, they decided unanimously, and with great joy, that the property should be given to the Daughters of Compassion for the orphanage. It seemed to everyone in the village to just be the right thing to do.

A week later, the orphanage moved into the ancient fortress beneath the violet beacon. Lady Elaine was ecstatic. The orphans were never wanting for food or shelter again. Litfim took it on himself to explore every nook and cranny of this new paradise he now called home. He spent long hours sitting up high in the tower, basking in the brilliant radiance of the Violet Light. People began calling him "the purple kid," since his skin had taken on a distinctly violet hue. Every morning, he would watch the sunrise from his perch up on the highest part of the tower, and dream of the day he would fight for King Tavon in the Darklands far to the east. Anskar was always nearby keeping a watchful eye, just in case he got a little too close to the edge of the platform.

CHAPTER 41

The Way Home

Sasha found herself walking through a deep, narrow canyon. She was all alone and wearing her old, tattered gypsy dress. Her sword was in a scabbard that hung over her shoulder. It seemed to weigh heavy on her back. A soft light filtered down through the trees high above. The path under her feet was rocky and uneven, and she found it difficult to walk without twisting her ankles. The trail meandered back and forth, and it got narrower as she advanced.

She soon came to an ancient stone gate. It appeared to be rarely used by travelers. Vines had grown over the lettering across the top, so she stood on a large stone nearby and pulled them away. The words read: The Narrow Gate to the Narrow Way. Sasha jumped down off the rock and studied the opening. She thought it was probably just wide enough for her to squeeze through. She stood sideways and just managed to push herself through to the other side.

As she continued walking, the canyon became even narrower and darker. She unsheathed her sword, and a bright, violet light from the blade illuminated the path. She kept walking for quite a distance, until the walls seemed to be closing in on her. The light from her sword went out and she felt like the stone walls were squeezing the life out of her body. She screamed and closed her eyes when she thought she was going to be crushed.

When Sasha opened her eyes again, she found herself lying in a soft, comfortable bed. The pillows were just the perfect size and fluffiness. The sheets and the blankets felt like silk. She just wanted to lie there for a while, because the bed filled her with such perfectly serene pleasure. Birds sang sweetly in the trees outside her window. The fresh, clean scent of Ehadre-el flowers filled the air. She prayed, "This is heavenly. I never want it to end."

The sound of a hammer tapping outside her door made her sit up. When she opened her eyes, she saw what looked like home. She was in her gypsy wagon, only it was better than her wagon. All of her favorite things were there, but they seemed purer now. It was as if the old things she used to treasure were only shadows of the real things she saw before her now.

As she stood up, she realized that she was wearing her favorite dress. Like the wagon, it was also better than the white dress she remembered. The small marks and frays in the dress were gone. It was brighter and cleaner now. The old dress was gray and tattered compared to this one. Yet it was also the same dress somehow. There were all the embroidered stitches her mother so lovingly sewed. Not a single one was missing.

The hammer tapped on the wall outside again. When she opened the door, she glanced at a tall, handsome, bearded man with nails in his mouth and a hammer in his hand. He was fastening a sign to the outside of the wagon that read, *Sasha—Defender of Orphans and Widows.* "There!" he said as he hammered in the last nail. "It is finished!" He looked at Sasha and said, "Welcome home, Sasha!" Something about the carpenter seemed so familiar, but Sasha felt confused and overwhelmed. She just stared at the sign on the wall, trying to figure out where she was and what the sign meant.

A female voice nearby said, "Good morning, Your Majesty! Thank you again for everything! I can't thank you enough!"

"You're welcome, Hala. It's my pleasure!" the carpenter said looking in her direction.

Sasha looked over toward the woman as well. She was bowing to the carpenter and appeared to be no older than Sasha herself. Actually, she looked a lot like Hala's grand-daughter, Mara, but it was not Mara.

"Hala! Is that you?" Sasha said, as tears began to fill her eyes.

"Sasha! You've arrived!" the woman screamed for joy. She ran over to Sasha and gave her a big hug.

"Hala, is it really you? You look so young!" Sasha said in amazement.

"Yes, isn't it great! Praise the Highest One!" Hala shouted with her hands in the air.

"But how? I mean, what happened?" Sasha said looking more confused than before.

"Sasha, look around you. Don't you know where you are?"

Sasha looked out over a low wall into a glorious paradise that stretched out for as far as the eye could see. A crystal clear river flowed out of a lush, verdant garden at the center of the huge city. At the center of the garden was an immense tree. A brilliant light permeated everything, making the sun and the moon unnecessary. Its walls were transparent silver. Its streets shone bright gold. Its buildings were made out of colorful precious gems. Its gates were made of solid pearl. Exotic birds flew through its skies and were perched in all of its trees. Amazing animals she had never seen before scurried across the ground. "Where am I?" Sasha whispered through her tears, already knowing the answer.

"You would call it Ehadreon. Others call it the City of the Great King. Please feel free to call it home!" the carpenter said.

Tears welled up in Sasha's eyes and she began to shake as she realized where she was. "I'm not worthy of this!" she said falling to her knees. She began sobbing uncontrollably with her hands over her face.

The carpenter knelt down on one knee next to her. He lifted up her face and gently wiped away her tears. "Take heart, daughter of the Highest. No one is worthy of it but me. That is why I give it to you freely as a gift. If you earned it, you would never be able to enjoy it for all eternity!"

His eyes seemed to pierce right through her soul, yet they were filled with endless compassion. Those eyes, filled with the wisdom of eternal ages, told her she was loved beyond anything she could imagine.

Then she looked down at his hands. She took his hand in hers and turned it over. There was a scar on both sides. She suddenly realized who he was. "You're him!" she shouted. "You're *him*!" She held him as tightly as she could.

"Yes, Sasha! Who else would be the first to welcome you to my city?" King Tavon said smiling and laughing. "I promised you I will always be with you! Welcome home!"

Filled with awe, she took his hand in hers and kissed the wounds that had brought her to paradise. She felt as if her soul was overwhelmed with pure joy, wonder, and a sense of unworthiness all at the same time.

Then King Tavon stood up. Holding out his hand to Sasha he said, "Come, follow me." Sasha stood to her feet, and she took hold of his hand. "I want to you to see your reward."

"Reward? I'm not worthy of a reward, Your Majesty!" she said shaking her head.

"Here they are!" he said, as he pointed to a large crowd that had gathered together near her wagon. "Here is your joy—your crown!" Sasha looked up and she saw her parents and Hala and hundreds of others standing in a large group, smiling broadly and waiting anxiously to greet her. "They are all here because you loved them in my name!"

She smiled her brightest smile through her tears. All the sacrifices had been worth it—every single one. She loved being home.

CHAPTER 42

The Adventure Continues

The bells of a thousand prayerhouses rang out across Varden when the people saw the light of the violet beacon in the west. It gave those loyal to King Tavon great encouragement and hope. There were days of celebration all across every nation, especially among those fighting the Dragon's forces in the Darklands, far to the east.

A battle-weary warrior carried a torch into a pitch-black cave in the former kingdom of Lisendore. The meager light made his face appear to be even more haggard. When he came to a small group of men in the back of the cave, he said, "Your majesty, there's something you need to see."

The man he addressed had a deep scar down his left cheek. In many ways, he resembled Stang. He could have been his twin brother.

"What is it?" King Andelsar said, slowly rising to his feet.

"It's very good news, sir! Come and see."

All the men followed the warrior out to the cave's entrance, and he pointed toward the western horizon across the war-torn landscape. There in the night sky a bright, violet light shone in the far distance.

"Could it be the sunset?" one of the men said. "The light plays all kinds of tricks here in the Darklands."

"No," replied the warrior. "The sun set hours ago. Reports are coming in that the Violet Light has been rekindled! Our scouts have confirmed it. The Murastan has been found and the beacon has been relit!"

The men sent up a cheer and threw their swords in the air, praising the Highest One. Andelsar fell to his knees and wept with his hands covering his face.

* * * * *

Ebesian's five students, along with Mandar and Bensareon, sat on the deck of the *White Eagle*. It had been placed on the rails of the windship ramp in Sugstal waiting for the professor to arrive. They had all gotten up early that morning, because they were eager to find the next key and relight the next beacon. The students were all smiling and laughing, recounting stories from their recent adventure.

"The whole building blew up and I thought Jon was dead!" Tasca exclaimed with great exaggeration. "But then I saw him coming out of the smoke and rubble, coughing and crying, 'Mommy! Help me, mommy!'" She mimicked Jon staggering and holding one hand to his chest and the other in the air. All the students laughed.

"I didn't do that!" Jon protested with a smile. "I said, 'I'm okay! I'm okay! I don't need any help!'" Jon then flexed both his biceps in a mock muscle-builder's pose.

Gransen playfully threw the core of the apple he was eating at Jon's puffed out chest, and Jon shouted, "Hey! I'm telling the truth!"

Traven said, "I like Tasca's version better!"

Landron said, "So do I!"

"Mommy! Mommy!" Tasca repeated close to Jon's face.

"I never said that!" he protested again, and they all laughed.

"Where is our fearless leader?" Mandar whispered into the air, standing with his back to the students and looking over the stern railing. He paced back and forth for a while, and then he sighed and sat back down again.

Just then, Ebesian staggered in with his large bags in each hand and his sword across his back. He hobbled up the gangplank and dropped his bags on the deck with a big thud. Then he turned toward the students. They all smiled brightly at him and it made him feel guilty about his grumpy attitude, so he smirked back at them. They all laughed at his expression.

"I see you are all in a good mood today!" Ebesian said, straightening his overcoat. "That's good, because the road ahead is not going to be an easy one. The violet key was the least difficult to find and the least protected by the enemy. It's going to get harder from here on out."

Mandar rolled his eyes. He stood up next to Ebesian and whispered in his ear, "Remember, no wet blankets!" Then he stood back, raised one eyebrow, and looked at his old friend with a knowing look.

Ebesian started over. "You all did a fine job, and I want to commend you. I am proud of all of you. I really appreciate all you've accomplished. Praise the Highest One for this great victory!" He looked over at Mandar and raised his hands toward him as if he was offering him a gift.

Then Ebesian turned back toward the students and said, "We now have the first key."

All the students clapped and cheered. Ebesian motioned to Ben to stand up, and Ben got to his feet and stood next to Ebesian. Ben unsheathed his sword and held it in both hands for the group to see. The light of ancient runes danced along the violet-colored blade. Just beneath the hilt, the key had embedded itself in the metal. They all felt a renewed sense of dedication to King Tavon just standing in the presence of its light.

"We are far from finished with our quest, my friends," Ebesian continued. "There are six more keys to be found. One of *you* may become the guardian of the next key we find. The Cranistan, or the azure key, will not come to a proud fool, but only one who is truly wise. It will only be wielded by someone with a clear mind and a humble heart. Who will it be?"

All of the students looked very somber now, and no one dared to speak until Ebesian said, "Questions!"

Jon asked the question they were all thinking. "Where are we heading to next, professor?"

"We're going to the university town of Ostval. The wizards in their science department have convinced everyone this world came into being by pure chance and there is no Creator. We are going to give them tangible proof that they are wrong!"

"Well, at least it will be easy for us to blend in as students in Ostval," Landron said, "and I know some of the professors there."

"Good!" Ebesian replied. "Begin to plan and pray about the next stage of our adventure!" Turning to Bensareon, Ebesian said, "Let's get this thing in the air, Captain."

Stang and a lizard were hiding close nearby. They carefully watched what was happening on the *White Eagle*, and they were both already planning their next move.

"I have to follow them," Lacertus whispered in Stang's ear. "That key lead to the death of Sasha. Now they are going after more of them. The keys are powerful. They must be mine!"

Stang believed that Lacertus' words were his own thoughts, and he needed to act on them. So with the stealth of a thief, he crept back to the gypsy camp and began packing what he needed to go to Ostval.

Captain Bensareon called for the final preparations to be made, and the crew sprang to action. As he looked out over the stern railing he saw a sudden flash of blue light. Then he saw several lizards scurry off toward the northern village gate. Anskar emerged from the trees and stood in the middle of High Street. The engven raised his bright sword in the air and shouted, "For the glory of the Kingdom of Tavon!"

Ben raised his sword and a tear came to his eye as he shouted back, "For the glory of the kingdom that will never end!"

As Anskar ran into the woods after the enemy, Ben had a sudden realization. By the will of King Tavon, the engven had not only protected their departure—they had been protecting Ben throughout his life! Ben was now about to fulfill his destiny. He was the guardian of the Murastan!

— End of Book 1 —

A SNEAK PREVIEW OF

TANGIBLE PROOF

BOOK 2 OF THE KEYS OF EHADREON: THE AZURE KEY

In another place and time much like our own —yet quite different from our own— Follison the Brown sat in his laboratory performing his latest experiment. On each of his wrists, there was a dark orange manacle. A rusty, orange chain ran from one manacle to the other underneath his tattered shirt and brown lab coat. His lab was filled with beakers and flasks, all tied together with condensing tubes and hoses. Gas flames were lit under some of the flasks, and various colored liquids bubbled up and around through the tubes. One wall had large windows extending from the floor to the ceiling, flooding the room with the morning light. A large metal machine, generating bright flashes of light and sizzling discharges, sat in the center of the room.

Follison was quite proud of the fact that he was a world-renowned wizard, but he never paid much attention to his appearance. His once white lab coat was now stained brown, severely wrinkled, and dirty. His greasy, brown hair always stuck out in all directions. His beard usually contained the evidence of whatever meal he had eaten earlier in the day. His eyeglass lenses were spotted and grimy. He did not have time to think about such trivial matters as his looks. He believed he was about to change how everyone sees the world, by proving once and for all that a Creator was unnecessary for life to exist.

He had given up on his former experiments in alchemy, trying to turn straw or lead into silver or gold. Now he was trying to prove his latest theory. He believed that he could produce a living organism from a soup of various chemicals if he zapped it enough times with discharges from the machine in his lab. For months now, he had tried all kinds of different ideas to prove that he was right. Every time, all he ended up with was muddy, brown, lifeless goo. The brown and black glop from all of his experiments sat in countless labeled jars across the back wall of the lab. It made the whole room smell like an open cesspool.

Follison took a flask of liquid from the end of his long sequence of glassware and hoses. He carefully poured the liquid into a test tube and placed it inside the machine at the center of the room. He gleefully pulled a long handle on the side of the machine, and it started to emit a high-pitched whine. *It has to work this time,* he thought. The machine shot a small lightning bolt through the test tube and it exploded. It made an ear-piercing, grinding noise followed by a loud bang. Then it filled the lab with thick, black smoke. Cursing out loud, Follison ran over to the machine and threw some powder on the flames rising up from it. When the smoke dissipated, he bent over the machine and tried to find some of the remaining liquid so he could scrape it into a spoon. He carefully placed the little goo he could find on a glass slide, and he put it under a microscope. He focused the lenses and peered down at his creation. "Nothing! Nothing but mud!" He threw a nearby beaker against the wall and the glass shattered into hundreds of pieces.

For a while he sat with his elbows on the counter and his head in his hands. His experiments were not working out the way he had hoped. He was feeling very depressed and disheartened. *This has to work,* he thought. *This is my life's work. Everything depends on this! It has to be true! The alternative is just unacceptable!* He did not realize he was simply repeating the words of the viper hiding under the counter at his feet. The snake crawled up the stool Follison was sitting on, and it bit him in the back of the neck, near the base of his skull.

Its poison flooded his mind. Soon, Follison was feeling much more positive about his research again. He decided to try his experiment one more time.

Varden Eye, Sword, and Key Colors

VIRTUES	VICES
Violet = love and sacrifice	Yellow green = greed and selfishness
Blue = courage and faith	Yellow = cowardice and unbelief
Azure = wisdom and humility	Orange = foolishness and pride
Cyan = self-control and purity	Red = anger and lust
Jade = encouragement and edification	Rose = gossip and dissension
Emerald = perseverance and hope	Magenta = despair and hopelessness
White = goodness and restoration	Black = evil and destruction

To download a copy of the Varden Color Wheel, maps and other extras go online to sjcarlsen.com.

Cast of Characters

Andelsar

Heir to the royal throne of Lisendore. The Nekron conquered Andelsar's kingdom centuries ago, and the Dragon now occupies his throne.

Ansen

The owner of the windship yard in Sugstal. His sons are Bensareon and Nathan.

Anskar

One of the engven who serve King Tavon. He appears as a woodsman throughout the story.

Arboron

A wealthy businessman from the city of Babbelar who looks like a frog.

Avarusa

One of Histrionicah's friends who lives and shops in Babbelar.

Bensareon/Ben

A young windship captain who lives in Sugstal. He is Ansen's son and Nathan's brother.

Berk

A big, smelly, feeble-minded gypsy who is one of Stang's henchmen.

Bovina
Arboron's amiable and acquiescent secretary.

Calypso
A greedy gypsy woman who runs a fortune telling business with her
   daughter, Hexah.

Capitalo
The minister of finance and wealthiest man in Corasar. He is a ruthless businessman who has swindled hundreds of people out of
   their retirement savings.

Dragon, The
The ruler of the nekron, who appears to be more powerful than he
   really is.

Ebesian/Ebus
An old loremaster and professor who is leading his students on a
   quest to find the seven keys.

Eyepatch
A gypsy who is one of Stang's henchmen.

Gathes
The Head of the High Council and Jon's father.

Gransen
One of Ebesian's students, who has the gift of healing.

Gwynneth
A foolish princess from the royal house of Payton, who invites herself
   to travel with Ebesian's students.

Hala
An old gypsy widow who lives next door to Sasha.

Hexah
Calypso's daughter who tells fortunes by means of a nekron on her
back. Her real name is Melantha.

Highest One, The
One of the names for the Creator deity on Varden.

Histrionicah
Arboron's wife, who is known for her selfishness, greed, and exaggerated dramatic behavior designed to attract attention.

Jon
One of Ebesian's students, who is known for his natural leadership
abilities.

Lacertus
The nekron assigned the task of protecting the violet key. He appears
as a lopsided lizard throughout the book.

Lady Elaine
A middle-aged woman who gave up great wealth and privilege to run
an orphanage in Sugstal. She is the founder and leader of the
Daughters of Compassion.

Landron
One of Ebesian's students who has doctorates in chemistry and
physics.

Lawson
An intelligent lawyer who lives in Sugstal.

Lilypad/Lily
A leading nekron who pretends to be Histrionicah's innocent lap-
frog. Also known as Nefario.

Litfim
A young orphan boy who is known for his curiosity and getting into trouble.

Magnus
The generous owner of the *White Stallion* and Sasha's boss.

Mandar
Ebesian's lifelong friend and fellow loremaster.

Melantha
Hexah's real name which was given to her before the nekron attached itself to her back.

Nathan
A young windship navigator. He is Ansen's son and Bensareon's brother.

Nefario
The real name of the nekron who pretends to be Histrionicah's lap-frog, Lilypad.

Pleonexia
One of Histrionicah's friends who lives and shops in Babbelar.

Sasha
A twenty-year-old gypsy and orphan known for her generosity and her warm outgoing personality. She works as a waitress at the *White Stallion.*

Stang
An ex-pirate captain who now leads a band of gypsies, and is known for his ruthless vigilantism. He has a long scar on the left side of his face.

Storfim
An orphan who is Litfim's older brother.

Tasca
Ebesian's granddaughter and student who is a princess of the royal
house of Saren.

Tavon, King
The eternal and omnipotent creator and true king of Varden. He cre-
ated the seven keys and the engven as well. He is now preparing
Ehadreon—the Eternal City.

Telecon
A greedy, false teacher who is popular in Corasar.

Traven
One of Ebesian's students who has multiple degrees in the Lore.

Twins, the
Two powerful nekron who are chained together. They appear as twin
snakes in the story.

Viridan
A man who has been driven mad by the yellow-green key, and now
lives in a dilapidated mansion.

Wartvox
A nekron who follows Arboron everywhere he goes. He appears as a
large toad in the story.

Zendel
The Director of Teaching for the High Council, and Traven's father.

Glossary

Ansar. The nation to the south of Corasar. The High Council meets at its citadel in Ansar.

Babbelar. The capital city of the nation of Corasar known for its affluence and greed.

Bergen Fjord. The fjord that runs east-west on the southern border of Bergendore and the northern border of Corasar. It connects to the Spygren Fjord near Sugstal.

Bergendore. The nation to the north of Corasar, inhabited by vikings.

Corasar. The nation east of Spysar, south of Bergendore, north of Ansar, and west of Samar. Its capital is the city of Babbelar.

Corasarian. A native or citizen of Corasar, or something related to or characteristic of Corasar.

Cranistan, the. One of the seven keys needed to relight the beacons of Varden. This key magnifies either pride and foolishness or humility and wisdom. In its twisted form, it is orange. In its proper form, it is azure or sky-blue.

Darklands, the. The name of Lisdendore since it has been occupied by the Dragon and his forces. The nekron call it "Norgar."

Ehadreon. The City of the Eternal King, which will one day replace all kingdoms on Varden.

Ehadre-el. Small violet flowers which show someone from Ehadreon has been present on Varden.

engven. Powerful, supernatural beings who serve King Tavon. In addition to other powers, they can teleport to any location, change their appearance at will, and perfectly blend into their surroundings. They appear as woodsmen in the story. The nekron are fallen engven.

fjord. A long, narrow, deep inlet of the sea between high cliffs.

High Council. The ruling body for all the prayerhouses throughout Varden.

keys, the seven. These are the keys that are needed to relight the seven beacons. Since they were forged in Ehadreon, they cannot be destroyed, but they can be misused. In their twisted form, the keys magnify negative or evil traits in people. In their proper form, they magnify positive or good traits. The Varden color wheel explains the opposite traits which each of the keys brings out of an individual.

krone. The basic monetary unit of Varden, literally meaning *'crown.'* The plural is *kroner.*

Lawson's Wood. The redwood forest to the north of the village of Sugstal. Not to be confused with the woods south of the village.

Light of Spysar, the. The lighthouse located in the northern edge of the village of Sugstal where the Bergen and Spygren Fjords come together.

Lisendore. The westernmost nation in Varden. Now known as the Darklands since the nekron now occupy and control it.

Lore. The prophecies, teachings, and historical account of King Tavon and his kingdom.

Lorebook. The written text of the Lore in book form.

loremaster. An expert in teaching the Lore.

Murastan, the. One of the seven keys needed to relight the beacons of Varden. This key magnifies either greed and selfishness, or love and sacrifice. In its twisted form, it is yellow green. In its proper form, it is violet.

nekron. Engven who have rebelled against King Tavon and become totally corrupted by evil. They appear as snakes, lizards, and frogs in Varden because they have become so corrupted by wickedness. They have the power to blend into their surroundings and tempt people by filling their minds with evil thoughts.

prayerhouse. A local meeting place for the teaching of the Lore and prayer.

rosemal. The art of painting wooden furniture and objects with decorative flower motifs.

Rothal. The capital city of the nation of Ansar, and the home of the Lore school where Ebesian is a professor.

Samar. The nation east of Corasar.

Spygren Fjord. The fjord that runs north-south on the eastern border of the nation of Spysar. It connects to the Bergen Fjord near Sugstal.

Spysar. The northwesternmost nation on Varden. It is the country where Sugstal is located.

Sugstal. A village perched on the eastern cliffs of the nation of Spysar.

Tavonian. Any person who serves King Tavon and is loyal to his kingdom, or something related to or characteristic of Tavon's kingdom.

Varden. The name of the world in which this story takes place. Varden was once verdant and filled with trees, but now it is a cold, dark, and dying world covered in snow and ice.

Vardenian. Any person living on the planet Varden, or something related to or characteristic of Varden.

violet. The color representing love and self-sacrifice on Varden.

windship. A boat with a triangular sail that can fly through the air or sail on the water. The sail is set horizontal for flight and vertical for sailing on water.

yellow green, The color representing greed and selfishness on Varden, also called chartreuse.

A Note from the Author on the Use of Biblical Texts

The student of Scripture will recognize that I have taken the liberty of quoting the Bible as if it was "the Lore" of the imaginary world I have created in this book. Although Varden and the characters in this story are fictional, I hope that the reader will see that the message of this story, and the Bible it is based on, are very real and true.

All biblical quotations are my own translations or paraphrases of the New Testament Greek text. Since it is my desire not to alter Scripture but to remain faithful to it, I invite the reader to look up the biblical texts used throughout this book and understand them in their proper historical and grammatical context. The footnotes give some of those references.

Hints to many biblical events, places, beings, symbols, and concepts are made throughout the book. I hope the reader will gain a richer, deeper understanding of Scripture by investigating all of these references. I also pray that the Author of the world's greatest book will be pleased with my feeble attempt to help others see how awesome His book truly is.

About the Author

Steven J. Carlsen has been a pastor for over thirty years. He is currently the lead pastor of a bilingual church, which reaches out to people of every nationality. He and his wife, Ruth, enjoy sailing and kayaking on the Jersey shore and the lakes of the Adirondack Mountains in New York. They also travel to Norway whenever they can to enjoy the beautiful fjords of this world.

CPSIA information can be obtained
at www.ICGtesting.com
Printed in the USA
FFOW02n0621240418
46360777-48019FF